"Why Are You Sitting All the Way Over There?"

"Why aren't you here, where you belong . . . ?" he questioned softly.

"Because we've tried, Jeff, but like oil and water, we just don't mix! Oh, we've had our moments, but then you say something, or I say something, and the sparks start flying again."

"Perhaps because we've tried everything but this . . ." He left the low leather chair to kneel on the floor in front of her. He bent nearer, and without reaching to hold her, touched his mouth to hers. "Forget the thousands of miles between here and Washington, real or imaginary," he whispered, kissing one corner of her mouth and then slowly caressing the other side, "and for once meet me halfway."

FRAN BERGEN

is a woman of many talents. She is fluent in Spanish and Italian and has also written numerous film scripts for some of the most popular shows on television. Ms. Bergen has traveled extensively throughout the United States and Europe. She currently resides in California.

Dear Reader:

SILHOUETTE DESIRE is an exciting new line of contemporary romances from Silhouette Books. During the past year, many Silhouette readers have written in telling us what other types of stories they'd like to read from Silhouette, and we've kept these comments and suggestions in mind in developing SILHOUETTE DESIRE.

DESIREs feature all of the elements you like to see in a romance, plus a more sensual, provocative story. So if you want to experience all the excitement, passion and joy of falling in love, then SILHOUETTE DESIRE is for you.

For more details write to:

Jane Nicholls
Silhouette Books
PO Box 236
Thornton Road
Croydon
Surrey CR9 3RU

FRAN BERGEN
Capitol Affair

Silhouette Desire

Originally Published by Silhouette Books
division of
Harlequin Enterprises Ltd.

*First published in Great Britain 1985
by Mills & Boon Ltd, 15–16 Brook's Mews, London W1A 1DR*

© Frances de Talavera Berger 1985

Silhouette, Silhouette Desire and Colophon are Trade Marks
of Harlequin Enterprises B.V.

ISBN 0 373 05191 3

22-0885

*Made and printed in Great Britain by
Richard Clay (The Chaucer Press) Ltd,
Bungay, Suffolk*

Other Silhouette Books by Fran Bergen

Silhouette Special Edition

Yearning of Angels
Prelude to Passion
Golden Impulse
Dream Feast
Perfect Harmony

For further information about
Silhouette Books please write to:

Jane Nicholls
Silhouette Books
PO Box 236
Thornton Road
Croydon
Surrey CR9 3RU

1

Stretching out her hand to take a glass of champagne from a gleaming silver tray, Monica Lewis didn't attempt to hide her curiosity as she looked about at the glamour that surrounded her that evening. She wasn't blatantly staring, of course, but she did allow herself a few candid glances over her slender shoulder. Yes, she mused, giving her long blond hair a gentle shake, this was definitely a very elegant affair. She was glad she was here.

The garden of the gorgeous Georgetown house was packed with "important" Washington types, only a few of whom Monica knew personally. Curiously, although she had been born and bred in the shadows of the Capitol, she had never yearned to take part in these chic politics-and-cocktails happenings while she was growing up. Her father, a venerated and respected judge—who was, nonetheless, sometimes irreverently referred to as "Somber" Lewis—frowned upon that sort of frivolity. He always swore that such gatherings were just an excuse for immoral "canoodling," as he quaintly called it, and he was loath to see his adored daughter tainted by such "loose socializing." Even after she left home to go to college, Monica hadn't become involved in the Washington social scene. Her family's lineage and prestige would have opened the doors to Washington's *crème de la crème,* but Monica had willingly avoided that side of the city's life-style in the past. Perhaps she had simply been too involved with getting a solid education and then applying herself to the rigors of law school to waste her time drifting from party to party; perhaps, later, she had been too highly motivated in her desire to succeed in her position as assistant director of the Youth in Government Foundation to allow herself time to relax for an evening on the town. Or perhaps, as her father always insisted, Monica was at heart a "damned maverick"—just as her mother and grandmother had been.

But this evening, Monica was thoroughly determined to enjoy herself. She had just made a daring professional move, and she was proud of herself for having taken the risk; tonight she fully intended to reward herself by kicking up her heels and having some fun, for a change. Glancing around the garden at the faces in the crowd, Monica assumed that most of the well-dressed guests were "regulars" who viewed fund-raising parties like this one as a necessary extension of political life in the nation's capital. Maybe she didn't fit that mold, but when a casual friend named Cissy, who also worked at the Youth in Government Foundation, called to invite her to the party, Monica had instinctively jumped at the chance to celebrate her future independence with a little lighthearted chatter, vintage champagne and some "loose socializing." As it turned out, the host and hostess, the Fairmonts, were old acquaintances of Monica's family—and that decided it.

Taking a sip of the perfectly chilled champagne, Monica continued to scrutinize the elegant crowd over the rim of her glass. She soon spotted Cissy across the garden, flirting outrageously with a hunky unmarried junior senator from the Midwest. A large palm enveloped the pair, affording them a hint of privacy, and Monica quickly glanced away. But Cissy suddenly threw her head back, laughing at something the young senator had whispered into her ear, and she spotted Monica. "Ah, Monica, come here," Cissy invited, waving and smiling across the lush garden. "Let me introduce you to my friend."

Monica set her glass down on a patio table and then walked slowly across the garden. She didn't especially want to meet Cissy's friend, but she didn't want to appear rude, either. "Hello," Monica murmured, putting a bright smile on her face and nodding to the pair.

"Are you having fun?" Cissy wanted to know.

"Yes, lots." As soon as the words were out of her mouth, Monica realized that this wasn't quite true. She was *trying* very hard to have fun, but so far—besides enjoying the champagne—nothing very lively had happened to her. Maybe she needed to relax a bit more, she thought, and be friendlier. "I'm glad I let you talk me into coming here tonight, Cissy." Monica's smile became dazzling. "Aren't you going to introduce me to your friend?"

Cissy looked as smug as a well-stroked cat. "Jack Smithfield, meet Monica Lewis." Sending Monica a secretive female-to-female wink—which actually could have been spotted with ease across the length of a football field—Cissy began to explain in a theatrical whisper, "Oh, Monica, I'm sure you know that Jack's the junior senator from—"

"Yes, of course I know," Monica interrupted, turning to look at the handsome politician. "Anybody who has eyes and ears knows Jack Smithfield. You're all over the media." She extended her hand. "It's very nice to meet you in person."

The junior senator seemed surprised by Monica's direct, unaffected manner, but he swiftly recovered. All smiles and charm, he began to retell the slightly ribald little joke which had given Cissy such glee only a few moments ago, this time for Monica's benefit. She only half-listened while she took stock of his appearance. There was no doubt about it, the man was attractive, appealing and desirable. Monica could easily understand why Cissy, possessively clutching Jack Smithfield's arm, was all aglow. After all, here in Washington politicos were worshiped as much for their charisma and sex appeal as for their politics and public status. Tomorrow, everybody who was anybody would be talking about pretty little Cissy Somebody-or-other who had caught Jack Smithfield's roving eye . . . and everybody would be wagering on how long it would take for Jack's eye to roam to another Ms. Somebody-or-other. . . .

Sex and politics were the standard bedfellows of life in Washington, but that was one pitfall Monica was vehemently determined to avoid. Although she had always remained on the outside fringe of the smart set, Monica knew many women, both close friends and casual acquaintances, who had eagerly rolled in and out of bed with public figures merely to fulfill a sexual fantasy or advance a career. That was all well and good, but Monica didn't wish to live *her* life that way. She had brains and she had pride, dammit. She also possessed all the natural healthy desires of a normal woman, but even so, she turned her back on the idea of advancing her career through sexual "credits." Maybe it was foolish, but that was the only way she could function. One of the main reasons she yearned to leave Washington was that she felt stifled by the all-consuming politics-and-sex rat-race atmosphere of the city.

Cissy laughed suddenly and so did Jack Smithfield. Slightly embarrassed, Monica realized that the senator had just delivered the punch line to his little joke. She recovered and quickly joined in the laughter, although for the last few minutes she hadn't heard a word he had spoken. She continued chatting with the pair— until she saw a chance to make her escape. "I'll see you later, Cissy, and it was really nice to meet you, Senator."

Leaving Cissy to eagerly reentwine herself in Jack Smithfield's arms, Monica walked away with a determined step. Once she was a safe distance across the large garden, she began to move aimlessly through the congested, chattering crowd. Suddenly annoyed with herself, she wondered what had happened to her earlier resolve to kick up her heels and have some fun at this party. What was wrong with her?

Just then, a waiter walked by with a tray of glasses. More champagne? Why not? It might help lighten her mood. Lifting a glass off the tray, Monica first took a deep breath, and then took a long sip of the wine. At that moment, a loud burst of welcoming laughter caused her to turn her head. She closed her eyes for a moment, and when she opened them again, she found that she wasn't hallucinating. Oh, it was true, all right—Jeff MacKennon had just walked onto the terrace.

In her fervor to attend the party, Monica had pushed to the back of her mind the very real possibility that she would meet Jeff MacKennon here. Now, too late, she realized how naive she had been to harbor the improbable hope that she would never see him again. Earlier, when she'd decided to attend the party, Monica's rationale had been that she and Jeff Mac-Kennon would miss each other in the crowd, or that she would probably leave the party long before he arrived, or that, by a miracle, he might even decide to skip this particular gathering. But no, there he was, looking every bit as gorgeous and self-confident as ever, damn him.

Monica suppressed a groan. Beneath the soft glow of small overhead lanterns, Jeff's black hair shone like jet-fire. And to make matters worse, it was almost sinful the way the lights brought out the silver flecks which highlighted those demonic dark waves. How on earth had she fooled herself into believing that he wouldn't make an appearance at this high-class bash?

"Is *that* your friend?" Cissy's voice hissed over Monica's shoulder.

Monica glanced around. "I wouldn't call Jeff Mac-Kennon a friend."

"But you do know him, don't you?"

"Yes, we met at a youth conference a few months ago."

Cissy smiled. "That makes sense. I mean, since you share a mutual interest in education." She somehow made the last word sound a little bit silly. "Do you two have anything else in common?"

"I told you, no."

"Well, I suppose that's fortunate, in a way."

Monica's eyes narrowed. Behind her, she could hear Jeff greeting people in a velvety voice. "What do you mean by that, Cissy?"

"I mean that Jeff MacKennon is bad news for serious little girls like you, my friend. He's a man on the way to the very top of the political ladder."

"I know all about it, Cissy." Monica kept her back stiff as a board, as if that would somehow ward off Jeff's presence. "I'll fill in all the details so that you can save your breath. Jeff MacKennon is a self-made man who is highly motivated to succeed. He's one of the brightest movers and shakers in Washington and he has everything going for him, from graduating first in his class at Harvard's Kennedy School of Government to escorting the most socially prominent females this town has to offer." Cissy appeared momentarily speechless, so Monica forged ahead—while she had the advantage. "He currently holds a high-powered position as director of program funding for an agency of the Department of Education, but rumor has it that he really has his eye on a high-ranking position at the White House." Monica smiled and tilted her head so that she could look straight into Cissy's surprised, wide-open eyes. "There, did I leave out any of Mr. MacKennon's amazing statistics?"

Cissy recovered fast. She looked hard at Monica and then smiled slyly. "For somebody who doesn't choose to run around in Washington's gossipy social circles, my dear Monica, you sure know a lot about Jeff MacKennon."

"As you said," Monica countered, with equal aplomb, "we share mutual professional interests and I can't help hearing what people say about him, that's all."

Cissy decided to be a good sport about Monica's one-upmanship. She laughed and shook her head. "Well, you were certainly right about Jeff MacKennon being the sex symbol of the century in this town. Rumor has it that to get anywhere with him a woman has to take a number and get in line!"

"Well, the competition has nothing to fear from me," Monica stated, laughing, "because I have something much more important on my mind at the moment than salivating over somebody like Jeff MacKennon."

"Oh?" Cissy was clearly unbelieving. "Are you sick or something? What in the hell could be more important than stalking somebody as delicious-looking as Jeff MacKennon?"

"Believe it or not, Cissy, I think there is something more important."

"Such as what, for God's sake?"

"I've applied for a new job in California—and I want it, desperately."

Cissy looked shocked. "California? What the heck would you be doing in California?"

Monica hesitated; just two weeks ago, Jeff MacKennon had asked her the exact same question. Oh, it had been phrased differently, but basically, the inquiry had been the same. "I need a change, Cissy."

Cissy made a face. "A change? Who would want a change from this?" She waved a delicate hand around at the glamorous crowd. "I think you're crazy! What would you do in California?"

"I would be heading my own department in youth education, instead of just being an assistant as I am here. It would be a wonderful step forward in my career."

Cissy appeared a little more concerned. "You're serious about this, aren't you?"

"I am."

"Is it a sure thing? The new job, I mean."

Monica tried not to look too worried. "Unfortunately, no, not yet. My application is still being considered at the Department of Education in Sacramento. But I'm hopeful."

"Well, it takes all kinds of lunatics to run this world, I suppose," Cissy said, sighing. "Are you really sure that's what you want?"

"I've never been so sure of anything in my life."

"Okay, I believe you," Cissy conceded, after taking a close look at the determined expression on Monica's face. "But just in case you should come to your senses and change your mind about skipping out to California, please be very careful if you suddenly decide to join in the competition for Jeff MacKennon." Cissy looked as if she were about to add something else, maybe something gentle and kind, but she swiftly overcame the weakness. "Well, just be careful, that's all."

"Don't worry," Monica insisted, "I would never stand in line for anybody, not even Jeff MacKennon. I'm not that crazy." Jeff's voice, floating through the garden, suddenly prompted her to ask, "But what about you, Cissy?"

"What about me?"

"Shouldn't *you* be more careful about involving yourself in sexy high jinks with ambitious politicians?"

"If you mean my blooming involvement with Jack Smithfield . . ."

"That's exactly what I mean. Cissy, you could get hurt, too, you know."

"Not me." A smug grin appeared on Cissy's face. "I know the rules of the game and I never allow myself to get hurt. Jack Smithfield is new to Washington and he's still awe-struck. He hasn't even begun to set his sights as high as Jeff MacKennon has. That'll take a while yet. For now, the two of us are enjoying a little fun, okay? In time, when he begins to climb, then I'll kiss him good-bye without tears or fuss, and I'll just find myself another junior senator, that's all."

Monica blinked, hard. "Forgive me, Cissy, but that sounds very cynical to me."

"Maybe, but I'm a realist and I want to have all the fun I can." She laughed, and it was a very brittle sound. "But that's enough gloom and doom! I really came over to tell you that Jack and I are leaving to have a little party of our own. You don't mind taking a cab home, do you? I mean, I feel rotten about leaving you in the lurch after driving you here . . ."

"No, Cissy, I don't mind," Monica assured her, actually feeling a tiny bit relieved about the way things had turned out. Cissy was shrewd; she had quickly guessed that Jeff MacKennon was not just a casual acquaintance. . . . "I'll call you."

"Oh, yes, do."

Cissy hurried away and Monica finally turned around to gaze at Jeff MacKennon. Oh, yes—in comparison, Jack Smithfield really was a raw beginner! She watched, fascinated by his technique, as he graciously shook hands with the men and kissed the women. As always, his entrance snatched attention away from everyone else—including the blond, blue-eyed movie actress who, until Jeff MacKennon arrived, had been holding court on the terrace—and once again he held the limelight all by himself. Jeff MacKennon, the all-American success story come to life: rags-to-riches, self-made, excruciatingly attractive, bright. He had chosen politics as his arena, but could easily have been a superstar in any other form of show business. He was also Washington's most eligible bachelor. Small wonder that the city's hostesses nearly trampled each other to snare him for their parties!

Monica relied on her common sense to get her through this awkward moment. She remembered that this could be the last time she'd see Jeff MacKennon for a long, long while. Maybe forever. If her luck held out, she would be leaving for California and a challenging new career in just a few weeks, so what did it matter if she was forced to face him one last time? She waited for the moment when he would finally see her. Outwardly, she looked serene and confident, but her mind was working at full throttle, grudgingly analyzing the impact this man had already exerted on her life. She struggled against it, but with startling swiftness, all the memories of the frustration and misery and hurt of their last encounter raced back to taunt her. Suddenly she felt her self-confidence ebbing, because she also remembered the infuriating excitement she had experienced throughout that unsettling evening two weeks ago. . . .

Jeff MacKennon had telephoned Monica that morning at her office at the Youth in Government Foundation. She wasn't particularly startled by his call because they had already shared several luncheons and dinners since their first meeting at a youth conference. Mostly, they had limited their discussions to education and budgeting for youth programs; both had seemed to be cautiously avoiding anything personal.

But at the sound of his voice on the line, she had felt a distinct interest stirring. "Have dinner with me tonight."

Monica hesitated. "Tonight?"

"Have you made other plans?"

"No, I haven't." Actually, she had put off washing her hair and doing her nails because she had been too tired the previous night to bother. Today she was convinced she looked a mess. And somebody wanted to take her out to dinner that evening, of all times. "No, I have no plans," she murmured again into the mouthpiece, critically surveying the tips of her nails where the polish was beginning to chip. She frowned at the sight. "Any particular reason for this sudden invitation?"

"None whatsoever, if you're referring to business. I just thought it would be very pleasant to take you to dinner at a lovely old inn I know."

Now her interest was even more aroused. "Just a whim, huh?"

"I guess you can call it that." The laugh was soft and genuine. "But I'm glad I gave in to it."

Very interesting, she thought. "And this lovely old inn, is it here in Washington?"

"No, it's in the Virginia countryside. However, it's just a short ride."

"Mm-m-m," she murmured, with just the right amount of lightness in her voice, "a secluded inn in the lush Virginia countryside!" Her tone remained light as she voiced her thoughts. "That sounds rather romantic to me, Jeff MacKennon."

There was a short silence before he answered. "I'm glad you finally noticed, Monica Lewis."

So there it was at last: the open invitation and the

provocative challenge, both at the same time. Their relationship had been casual and relatively uncomplicated until that point, although each was aware of the other's considerable attractiveness—why start something now? "Just in case you've forgotten, I'll probably be leaving Washington in a few weeks." She felt compelled to remind him. They had talked about her move, although not at great length. "Would it be wise to have this *tête-à-tête* in the charming countryside under the circumstances?"

"Why not?"

"I could give you a long list of reasons why we shouldn't, Jeff. For starters—"

"Forget the excuses, Monica, because I still want to see you. What's wrong with having a wonderful meal together, with superb wine and . . . ?"

This was Jeff MacKennon at his most persuasive and charming, Jeff MacKennon at his best—impossible to resist. Why not have dinner with him? But first she forced herself to be reasonable and logical. "And of course, you won't try to talk me out of going to California, will you?" she questioned.

"I'll try not to talk about your flight from civilization to the hinterlands, but I can't swear to it."

"In that case, Jeff . . ."

"Oh, come on, Monica, don't be so mean to me." His voice grew softer with each syllable. "We'll spend the evening indulging ourselves in interesting conversation between two mature, intelligent people. Doesn't that sound good and safe to you?"

The plain truth was that Jeff MacKennon had made

up his mind about something, and Monica was unable to tell him no. "I give up! All right, I'll have dinner with you," she said, laughing, "and we'll have a wonderful night of sparkling, brilliant conversation."

"Thanks." He seemed delighted, not triumphant. "Now, you told me that you usually work late, so shall I stop by for you at your office, say . . . at seven?"

She gazed down at her nails. "Here . . . at seven?" Just then, she felt a tiny, feathery sensation along the length of her leg, and she knew that if she glanced down, she would find a long run in her panty hose. That did it. "No, I won't be working late tonight." Monica ignored the look of surprise on the face of a coworker standing nearby, with whom she had discussed working late into the night on an important program only a few minutes before Jeff's call. "Why don't you pick me up at my apartment, instead? Seven will be fine."

Monica hung up and closed her eyes for a moment. There was plenty of time, she told herself. It was not quite four-thirty, and she had plenty of time to get ready. After promising her coworker that she would be in the office early the next morning to go over the notes for the program, Monica grabbed her purse and ran to her car.

She reached her apartment in the Foggy Bottom district in near-record time because she had beaten the rush-hour traffic. Once inside, she hurriedly looked around; everything was neat and orderly. Before rushing into the shower, she started a fire in the stone fireplace and then poured herself a glass of wine.

The clock on the mantelpiece chimed; it was five o'clock. She still had plenty of time to get ready. Maybe she would wear something new, something slinky, something *special*. Maybe that new silver-and-black beaded top, she pondered—and then she stopped herself in mid-thought. What was she doing? Why was she working herself into a tizzy because of a casual dinner date? Even though the man was Jeff MacKennon, this was no way to carry on. True, he was famous and very attractive, but Washington abounded with charismatic men—so what was the big deal about Jeff MacKennon? He certainly wasn't the first extraordinary man she had known—her husband had been handsome, gregarious and quite extraordinary in some ways—so why was she suddenly fretting about what she should or shouldn't wear this evening? The heck with it! She would wear her lovely but old silk dress to dinner with the much-admired Mr. Mac-Kennon, and that was that!

Two hours later, at precisely seven o'clock, Monica walked to the French windows and pushed aside the drapes. No sign of Jeff yet. She absentmindedly smoothed down the hem of her dependable dress while peeking down at her stockings and shoes. The sandals were new and very fragile-looking, but she had decided to wear them because of the high heel. Jeff MacKennon was quite tall and she felt more secure, somehow, in feeling slightly taller herself this evening. When the doorbell rang, she jumped. Had she been so preoccupied that she hadn't noticed his car drive up? "Hello," she said as she opened the door. "You're very punctual."

Jeff remained framed in the doorway. "You sound surprised."

"Nobody is ever on time in Washington."

"I'm the exception, then." A half-smile lit his face. "And so are you, it seems. I like the way you look."

His admiring gaze moved from head to toe, vanquishing the last doubt she might have had about wearing the dependable silk. "Thank you." She smiled, welcoming him with a wave of her hand. "Can I get you something to drink?"

"No, thanks."

He strolled to the center of the combination living-dining room, looked around, and then nodded. "Very nice."

"I'm glad you like it." She cast a fond glance around her home. "The place is a converted carriage house and it's really too expensive for me, but I love it."

He took his time looking at the beautiful old polished hardwood floors, the stone fireplace and the high French windows. His eyes flicked over the tasteful, expensive furnishings, missing nothing of their cost and value. "That's a strange thing for a member of one of Washington's most established families to say." He seemed to be talking to himself. "I would think that you could afford anything you wanted."

"This may shock you, Jeff, but since I decided to strike out on my own without my family's help, nobody has paid my bills but myself. I work for a living."

He broke the rising tension with an apologetic smile. "So do I—so relax." But then his expression shifted to something less friendly. "They build houses differently in California, you know. Your tastes will have to change."

She continued to gaze across the hushed, dimly lit room into his eyes, the largest, most intriguing eyes she had ever seen. "I think I'll cope."

"Oh, yes, I'm sure you will."

So, she mused, it was going to be a difficult evening, after all. She would have preferred a pleasant evening, one which would end in a friendly and gentle good-bye. . . . "Well, if you won't have a drink"—her purse and silk shawl were on a side table and she slowly gathered them into her hands—"should we be on our way?"

The drive across the Potomac and then along the George Washington Parkway into Virginia was made in almost total silence. Once, looking out the car window, Monica noticed that the trees and occasional houses looked eerie in the hazy darkness. The air was heavy, and it felt like rain. "Are you cold?" she heard Jeff ask. "No," she told him, "I'm fine."

The inn was everything Monica had expected. It was beautifully old and delightfully secluded. They dined superbly in the eighteenth-century elegance of the Georgian Room, a showplace crowned by wooden beams and lighted by beeswax candles in pewter sconces. Talk was about generalities and Monica admired the way Jeff could make the most trivial story sound interesting. But then, why not? He was a public personality, used to talking to people, comfortable in the glare of press conferences as well as in more private political arenas.

Finally, coffee was served. As they sipped the steaming liquid, Monica noticed a subtle but tense shift in the atmosphere. When Jeff spoke again, his tone was different. "You shouldn't be thinking about leaving Washington, Monica. It's an irrational idea."

"I don't think so." She didn't like his pedantic statement. "Besides, you promised you wouldn't bring that up."

His eyes sparkled with a hint of exasperation. "Why not? Is it something sacred or sinful which shouldn't be discussed, or even mentioned?"

"Jeff, we've been through this before, haven't we?"

"No, we haven't."

"Oh, yes, we have. I told you that I had made up my mind to apply for that job in California."

"And I advised you against such a move, but we've never talked about the *reasons* why we each feel the way we do, have we?"

"I don't see why it's necessary to delve into my reasons for doing anything," she said heatedly. "I'm old enough to make my own decisions."

He shrugged away her sarcasm with ill-concealed impatience. "Monica, your talents have been wasted at the foundation; everybody knows that. All right, you've done your 'bit for mankind' and you've paid your dues by helping gifted high-school students receive academic credit while working in various branches of the government, and I totally agree with you that you should move on to some other type of work, something more challenging. What I don't understand is how you can trade the excitement and vitality of Washington for a political backwater like

Sacramento, for God's sake! Your future, your family, your friends—your whole life—is here in Washington, not in some provincial state capital."

"Provincial?" He had succeeded in provoking her, and even though she resented the impulse, she fought back. "May I remind you, Jeff MacKennon, that Sacramento is the capital of California and can hardly be written off as a hick town."

He leaned across the table. "Maybe, but that still doesn't explain why you're running away."

"That's a cheap shot, Jeff." Now she was leaning closer to him, also. "I'm not running *away,* I'm running *toward* something new and stimulating. I want to advance my career and I want a new life-style—"

He quickly interrupted her last remark. "What's wrong with the way you live your life here in Washington?"

"There's nothing wrong with it—it's just not what I want. I'm not interested in the political social whirl, that's all."

He gazed at her closely while trying to interpret the full meaning beneath her words. "You surprise me. With your impeccable background, you should be very happy here in Washington." Something dark passed across his features, hardening them. "Some of us haven't been that lucky." His tone was cynical. "However, finding influential friends in this town is very easy."

So he was touchy about his background, Monica realized. Perhaps the hard climb from rags to riches had left some scars, after all. "I've told you that I don't rely on my family or friends for anything. I suppose

I'm considered overly independent, but I don't care what others think. As for the social set and all their parties . . ."

"Don't tell me you're antisocial," he quipped.

"I'm not." She lifted her cup and drank some coffee. The rich brew tasted good and strong. "My father disapproved of 'loose socializing,' as he called it, and I suppose some of that philosophy has rubbed off on me."

"Ah, yes, Judge Lewis . . . sometimes called 'Somber' Lewis, right?"

He was teasing to lessen the tension and she went along with it. "There's nothing 'somber' about me, believe me. I enjoy being with people, really being with people—talking, exchanging ideas, sharing things, and not just smiling and waving across jammed rooms filled with near-strangers." She glanced up at him. "Jeff, can you understand what I mean?"

"You prefer a one-on-one experience."

She was no longer amused by his teasing. "Sometimes," she snapped, "but maybe because of *my* background, I've been extremely selective." He got the message and she watched his dark eyes narrow. Then, a moment after, she felt rotten about it. Stay away from the personal, she reminded herself, never meaning to wound him so deeply. "As for my career," she said, quickly changing the subject, "I don't know why you, of all people, can't understand that I want to head my own staff—and I can do that in Sacramento —rather than being an assistant in Washington all my life."

When he finally spoke, his face was impassive, but

his voice was edged in skepticism. "Everything you've told me sounds reasonable on the surface, but there's something wrong with your arguments. Somehow, you've failed to convince me, Monica."

Still upset with herself for slashing at him, she tried a joke to lighten the mood. "Well, who said that it was better to rule in hell than serve in heaven?"

He also stopped to savor the coffee before answering. "Milton gave that line to Satan, but I don't happen to agree with his philosophy—just as I don't happen to agree with yours. I refuse to settle for second-best, no matter what it's called." He settled back with ease, caught the waiter's eye and ordered a brandy for himself—Monica had declined the after-dinner drink —and then he went on to explain, "I would prefer to remain in heaven and battle for the top job until I won." He paused while the brandy was brought to the table. When they were alone again, he lifted his glass and then swallowed some of the amber liquid. "So should you, Monica. If you want a change in careers, I think you should remain in Washington and pursue the occupation you were trained for—the practice of law. You would do better to stop being so damned independent and let your father assist you in establishing a law practice. Or," he murmured, "are you actually afraid that you might not be able to cut it as a lawyer in the nation's capital?"

They were even now. She took the jab with her chin held high, and then immediately came back. "I have complete faith in my brains and capabilities, Jeff MacKennon. Also, you should know that I don't scare easily."

"Then why don't you use your brains instead of wasting yourself on penny-ante positions in education, especially in Sacramento?"

"Someday I'll turn to practicing law, but right now I'm interested in and totally committed to programs for the gifted youngsters of the nation. California will offer me a great career challenge, but mainly I pray I get the job because I love working with the youngsters. I don't happen to believe that educating the future generation is penny-ante stuff—I happen to think it's one of our most important priorities." She saw the expression on his handsome face and she felt the urge to knock him on his rear. "Go ahead, smirk and call me an idealist, but I'd rather be an idealist than a cynical opportunist . . ."

"We weren't discussing *me,*" he countered smoothly. "I know exactly where I'm going after I'm through with education and I know exactly when I'll make the move. But your problem's different."

"You know, you're getting me angry." Monica was exasperated. "What difference does it make to you what I do with my life? We met by accident at a conference only a few months ago and we have absolutely nothing in common but our line of work. It's not as if I were your protégée or something, is it? Why should you give a hoot in hell if I stay in Washington or go to Sacramento . . . or even Timbuktu, for that matter?"

He slowly leaned forward in his chair. "You're very intelligent, so I can't accuse you of being dense, Monica." He regarded her thoughtfully for a moment, and a gentle smile tilted the corners of his mouth.

"And in case I haven't mentioned it before this, I also think you're a very beautiful woman."

"Thanks," she replied, dryly polite, "but I don't think that's a fair way to stray from the point."

He looked amused. "Can you think of a better way to stop an argument?"

"Yes, I can," she responded. "We can call it a night and you can drive me home. Period. End of argument."

"Strangers might do that, but . . ."

"Come on, Jeff, we're not what you would call close friends!"

"Oh, it's true that we spend most of our time together casually talking about subjects like educational problems or the lure of wanderlust," he murmured with a smile, "but don't lie to yourself, Monica—we're not strangers anymore."

All of a sudden, she felt a little defeated. Okay, so the way he was looking at her was anything but indifferent. She herself was beginning to feel a tiny telltale stirring under the gaze of those incredible eyes. But, dammit, that silly tingle was strictly biological—and reversible! "Don't push it, Jeff, it's hopeless. I'm very flattered, but I'm not interested."

"If you say so."

"I mean it." How could she convince him that, aside from her very real urge to put down roots somewhere else, they could never be compatible because of their backgrounds and future ambitions? How could she say it nicely, without sounding snobbish or pompous? "We're just too different in every way, too strongly different, Jeff."

"I agree, don't worry." The way he said it—so smoothly, so evenly, so matter-of-factly—would have fooled anybody less perceptive than Monica. "But what does that have to do with you and me at this moment?"

"Everything! We have opposing values . . ."

"I don't buy it. You talk about 'fairness' and 'values' and I want to talk about you and me and something pushing us together."

"Jeff, please shut up." They had been sitting at the table for a long time, and the dining room was almost deserted. Only a few waiters remained, standing discreetly in the background. Monica looked down at her empty coffee cup and concentrated on following the pattern of gold filigree leaves embossed on the rim. "I don't want any entanglements in my life at this moment. I just want to be free. I don't think I could handle anything else."

"What if you didn't have a choice?"

She tore her eyes away from the intricate gold leaves. "But I *do* have a choice, don't I? Look, Jeff, after tonight, you'll go right on building your fabulous career until, someday, you'll walk into the White House. If I luck out and get that wonderful job, I'll be basking in the California sunshine for a long, long time. See, it will be that simple if we just say good night, good-bye and good luck."

"And if you don't land that job, what then?"

Monica had spent hours worrying and wondering about what she would do if that happened. Now, suddenly, with no doubt in her mind whatsoever, she knew what she'd do. "I'll go to California, anyway. I don't think I'll have too much trouble finding another interesting job—and I think it's high time I proved something to myself. Now, if you don't mind, I want you to drive me back to Washington."

The quiet vehemence in her voice surprised him. He nodded curtly and said, "All right, if that's the way you want it. I'll get your shawl from the cloak room."

Monica was already on her feet. "Thanks. I'll wait outside."

2

When had it begun to rain? Monica wondered. A storm had finally broken loose from the cloud-covered skies, and she remembered thinking earlier that it would probably rain. She couldn't wait for Jeff outside or she'd be soaked, so she remained in the inn's quiet, empty foyer. She walked toward a tall mullioned window, and bending, pressed her forehead against the glass. It felt surprisingly cold; no, it was her skin that was startlingly warm.

Monica knew full well why she had practically run from the dining room. She was convinced that she wanted to get away from Washington; yet, for a moment back there as she had looked at Jeff in the muted candlelight, she'd felt a real regret at the turn of events. While it was true that Jeff MacKennon was many maddening things—overly self-confident, opinionated, a charming tormentor—he *had* hit the mark when he'd spoken of an emotional spark beginning to burn between them. But it wasn't the first time she had been more than casually attracted to somebody, and hopefully it wouldn't be the last.

Engrossed in thought, Monica was startled when Jeff wordlessly slipped her silk shawl around her shoulders. "Thanks."

He nodded and then moved to the front door. The rain was coming down in a gale and it was also ominously black outside. "I'm sure the country roads have turned into murderous mudholes in this storm." He glanced over his shoulder at her. "That thin shawl will be pretty useless—you'll be drenched the moment you step outside to get into the car." Then he turned again to stare straight into the wet night. "We'll be lucky to get back to Washington without having an accident."

She pulled the shawl more tightly around her shoulders. "Don't worry about me, I won't melt. I think we should chance it before it gets worse," she murmured, making a move toward the doorway.

But he was quicker, and stopped her. "But *I'm* not willing to chance it, Monica."

They were standing very close together and she could feel the warmth of his breath on her cheek. "What would you suggest we do instead?" she inquired, shutting her eyes for a moment to block his gaze.

"We could go to the bar and wait it out."

Stretching to look over his shoulder, she saw the glow of low, seductive lights at the other end of the foyer. The faraway sounds of soft laughter floated from the cozy barroom. Nice, she thought, but . . . "And if it should keep raining like this?"

"Then we have only one reasonable, logical alternative left, haven't we?"

"To spend the night here—together, you mean."

"Of course."

"Wrong." She took a step back, but he immediately closed the gap between them. "Look, Jeff—" But she came into contact with his mouth at that instant and the flow of words died in her throat. She tried to pull away, but he wouldn't let her, so she went limp for a moment before making another attempt to escape. Meanwhile, however, she was being kissed thoroughly; thoroughly surprising, also, was the fact that it was so enjoyable. It was too good to stop. Suddenly it didn't matter to her what people whispered darkly about Jeff MacKennon—that his allure and charm were practiced and superficial, or that beneath the smooth facade he was as hard and merciless as steel—because the only strength captivating her now was the grip of his arms and hands. He was holding her so tightly that she could imagine her bones snapping. Then she reached around to hold him, too, and moved her lips more experimentally against his, letting him freely explore and stroke the inside of her mouth. Too fast, she felt the excitement and the heat and the chill, all at the same time. . . .

Finally, he spoke. ". . . Stay with me."

"That's a terrible idea."

The tip of his tongue slid across her lips. "That doesn't make sense. . . ."

"It makes as much sense now as it did fifteen minutes ago."

He pulled back a little. "Okay, I may have said a few things that were out of line, and I'm sorry." He bent and caught her mouth again, breathing the words inside. "But I'd be crazy if I let you go so easily."

She let him play with her mouth a little longer. "Because"—her lips were swelling from the erotic playfulness—"of *this*, you mean?"

"Can you think of a better reason?"

So simple. From Jeff MacKennon's point of view, why shouldn't it be so simple? Monica eased herself back an inch or two just as another muted peal of laughter drifted from the bar. The cozy little room was probably packed with Washingtonians having a lark at the popular historic inn, and here she was, locked in Jeff's arms in a public foyer. By morning, whether or not they'd spent the night together, she would be just another statistic in the gossip columns! "Look, Jeff, I find you wonderfully exciting, but I'm not about to sleep with you—"

A burst of noise from the bar drowned the rest of her words, but Jeff thought he understood. "Nobody will know."

For some reason, his comment hurt. "You sound as if you speak from experience. Is this one of your favorite hideaways?" She saw the spark of annoyance that touched the dark eyes, but even so, she persisted. "A superb dinner, a smattering of bright conversation, and then a carefree night together? Is that the usual scenario?"

The angry spark was a little more pronounced now. "Sometimes."

"But with me, nobody will know. You guarantee it."

The expression in the dusky eyes suddenly became possessively sensual. "I promise." An irregular beat affected the soft laugh that followed. "Half the stories whispered about me are lies anyway."

"Then the other half must be true."

He shrugged away the importance of that small detail. "I'll take you into the bar, I'll order you a drink, and then you can wait for me there while I get us a room."

Monica could feel the silk of her dress slipping and sliding against her skin as his hands moved back and forth along her spine. When he pressed his fingers into the hollow at the small of her back, she experienced a small shock. Her surprise stemmed not so much from the fact that the intimate gesture created a pleasurable, arousing sensation down through her hips and beyond, but rather from the realization that they still stood in the foyer, and even though it was momentarily deserted, somebody could appear at any moment. She didn't relish being fondled in public, and the inference was unmistakable: he thought that only an insignificant amount of petty pawing was enough to get her to go to bed with him. She suddenly exploded, but in a dangerously quiet way. "Get your hands off me, Jeff."

He chose to ignore the warning. "I've wanted you since I first saw you."

"No." Taking direct action, she grabbed his wrists

and tore his fingers away from her body. "I'm not interested in a one-night stand."

"It doesn't have to be so cut-and-dried, Monica." He was at his most attractive this way, pleading and so softly adding pressure to his inducement. "There's always tomorrow and the day after. . . ."

"Dammit, you haven't taken seriously one word I've said to you tonight, have you?"

Monica stopped, not only because she was angry and completely exasperated but also because she saw that they were no longer alone. She hastily smoothed down her skirt and at the same time sent Jeff a direct warning with her eyes. Two couples had left the bar and were now walking across the foyer, laughing. They caught sight of Jeff and Monica and veered in their direction, smiling and waving; in fact, one of the men hailed Jeff by name and stopped to exchange a few pleasantries with him. Monica put a polite smile on her face. The couples speculated about the safety of driving back to Washington in the rain. Actually, the storm had lessened a fraction and the Washingtonians decided to take the chance. They left, smiling and waving once again, leaving behind a strong, damp draft which flew in through the doors . . . and a very tense, though quiet, Jeff and Monica.

Finally she broke the silence. "Please take me home."

He risked placing his fingers very lightly on her shoulders. "Are you sure?"

"Yes. That's exactly what I've been trying to tell you all evening."

"Listen to me, Monica. I'm sorry that nothing

happened tonight. There's nothing wrong with two people having good memories of each other."

"I don't want memories of you," she countered in a deliberately flat voice. Actually, her throat was hurting from the effort it took to speak quietly and calmly. She tried to ease the feeling by speaking more lightly. "Anyway, I would hate to think I left behind any gossip which could reach my father. You haven't forgotten my father, have you? He's the one you called 'Somber' Lewis, remember?"

For the first time, Jeff looked uncomfortable. "I shouldn't have said that, mainly because I admire and respect his work very much." His face darkened and his features seemed sharper, more accentuated. He was very frustrated, but at the moment he was also uptight about the blunder concerning her father that had slipped through his usual control. "It was a bad mistake, and I apologize."

"This whole evening has been a mistake, Jeff—for both of us," she admitted, turning to lean on the door. "I want to go now."

"All right." After hesitating for a moment, he held the door open for her, but his face was set in a blank mask. She gathered her shawl around her body and then passed through the doors without looking back.

He left her at her Foggy Bottom apartment door without touching her again; in fact, he seemed determined to avoid any contact with her, even when he took the keys from her hand to politely unlock the apartment door. Monica's mood had changed from anger to depression on the dreary ride back into Washington. Now she couldn't let him leave with only a mumbled good-bye. "Do you still refuse to understand why I couldn't stay with you tonight?"

"Does it matter what I think?" The smile on his lips was tight and forced. "Anyway, you'll be in Washington a few more weeks yet, no matter what happens with your new job. This is good night, not good-bye."

"We probably won't see each other again."

"Then I'll call to say good-bye."

He began to walk away. "Jeff . . . ?"

He turned around. "I didn't think there was anything left to say, Monica."

"There is." Somehow, she had to make him understand. "If I weren't planning to go away, I think I would have liked being with you tonight."

He remained cool and in control, but his sarcasm was evident. "Even though you're nothing but a sex object to me?"

"Stop it, Jeff."

"All right, now it's my turn to level with you. Do you think you can take it?"

Her chin shot up. "Try me."

"You're caught in a dilemma, Monica, and you don't know how to solve it. You're damned attracted to me, but you've stuck your neck out about working in California and you're too much of a spoiled brat and a maverick to admit that just maybe you've made a mistake. You're the type of woman who will never admit you could possibly be wrong about anything."

"So that's how you see me." She spoke with a swift snap of her head and flint in the blue eyes. "You just write me off as a brat and a maverick, is that it? Don't you think I also have plans for my life—just like you do? Jeff, I don't want everything turned upside down because I've met somebody like you. Do you understand?"

"I think so," he said, "but you've left out something very important."

She blinked. "What?"

"You don't know how I feel about you." He smiled, but it was quizzical, not complacent. "Maybe I'm not sure, either. We both might have found out tonight— but it's too late now." He turned and strolled toward his car. "I'll call to say good-bye, Monica."

Now, two weeks after that evening in Virginia, Monica watched Jeff MacKennon walking deliberately toward her, a puzzled look on his handsome face. Suddenly, for Monica, everything else—the riot of hot-pink flowers that covered the terrace, the beautiful people sipping perfectly chilled champagne and the lovely Georgetown garden—all blurred into the background. She had been shocked by the last words he had flung at her that night two weeks ago. They still burned and irritated her mind, and she felt the resentment rising to tighten her throat. But whether the resentment was directed toward Jeff or toward herself, she wasn't quite sure.

He was standing very close to her. Ignoring the sly glances that followed his every move, Jeff bent his head slightly to the side and brushed a kiss across Monica's lips before she could stop him. "I was going to call you tomorrow morning," he assured her so that only she could hear. "Any news from the wild west about that job?"

"Not yet," she was forced to admit, "but I'm sure I'll hear something soon."

"From the way you said that, I gather you haven't changed your mind about leaving Washington."

"No, I certainly haven't."

"Monica, do yourself a favor and smile at me, won't you? Try to be congenial and pleasant—everybody's watching us, you know." He was taking delight in teasing her again. "You wouldn't want to tarnish your reputation before leaving town, would you?"

She grudgingly admired his nerve. "I'm always congenial and well-behaved in public, or have you forgotten that, Jeff?" However, as much as she hated to do it, she did smile, sweetly and innocently. "There, is that better?"

He let her sarcasm pass. "I thought you never came to parties like this. Any special reason for coming to this one?" Before he could go on to add anything else, he inclined his head to catch a little comment whispered in his ear by their hostess, Marion Fairmont, as she fluttered by. After laughing in just the right, light tone at the elegant woman's jest, he immediately turned his attention back to Monica. "Tell me, why *are* you here?"

Now, that was a very good question, Monica realized. It was a question she thought she had answered quite satisfactorily earlier in the day when Cissy had called to invite her to the party. But now, face to face with Jeff once more, she acknowledged the fact that she hadn't been altogether truthful with herself. For one thing, although she felt jubilant about a new future in California, she still hadn't heard a word from

Sacramento; for another, quixotically, maybe she had hoped to see Jeff MacKennon just one more time. If that were true, then she was really asking for trouble. If she allowed herself to become involved with Jeff, her future could turn into an entangled, insane, unsolvable emotional mess. . . .

Meanwhile, of course, Jeff was still waiting for an answer. There was nothing left to do but carry on with all the poise and self-confidence she could muster. "I told you, I'm not antisocial."

"But you are gun-shy in a one-on-one situation, if I recall," he teased.

Her temper began to stir. "There's no use going on with this conversation. Good-bye." She whirled about and took off across the garden. When she reached the protection of the large palm recently vacated by Cissy and Jack Smithfield, she suddenly found herself grasped from behind. "Jeff, for goodness' sake, don't make a scene! Let go of me," she hissed, glancing around frantically to see if anybody had noticed them. She saw Marion Fairmont, one elegant eyebrow raised, gazing at them for a moment before she turned and continued to make conversation with a swarthy diplomat in a dashing salmon-hued turban. "Why don't you just leave me alone?" Monica pleaded.

Jeff laughed, grasping her a little harder. "On the contrary, I was about to suggest that we find someplace where we could be alone together." He seemed to be contemplating the problem. "I know . . . come on."

Monica couldn't protest too loudly because they'd attract more attention, so she was forced to follow Jeff, mainly because he held on to her hand with an iron grip. They wound their way along the edge of the garden until they entered the house through a high terrace door. They were in the library, and it was altogether lovely. It had been decorated completely in white—bookcases, walls, drapes, everything—with only massive amounts of leather-bound books to lend a contrast in color. The large room was subdued and inviting. It was mantled in darkness; the only light came from an ample colonial-style fireplace stacked with flaming logs. "Nobody will bother us here, and you can shout at me as much as you want."

"I don't shout in public," Monica said, feeling manipulated and frustrated.

"But we're not in public now," he reminded her, "so go ahead, do or say anything you want . . . if it'll make you feel better."

She had calmed down, however, and his words left her unrattled. She eyed the large double doors, but quickly changed her mind about making an escape, since he would probably reach them before her, and he could easily stop her from leaving the room. Instead, she gazed around the library as if she were really fascinated by its contents; in fact, she gazed at everything but him. Finally, to fill in the awkward gap, she murmured, "You seem to know your way around this house rather well. Are you and our hostess old friends?"

"Yes."

"I see."

"No, you don't 'see' at all."

"I just thought, since you said that it was easy for you to meet influential people . . ."

"Take that look off your face, Monica. Both Marion *and* her husband are solid *old* friends."

"Sorry, it's just so easy to jump to conclusions with your reputation," she murmured.

"Monica, why the hell don't you stop acting so childish?"

"Fine," she said, smiling archly. "First you call me a brat and then a maverick and now you accuse me of being childish. What next?"

He was standing by the terrace door; he hadn't moved since they'd stepped into the room, but now he slowly started toward her. "How about 'sensual' and 'exciting'—or would you consider those words insulting, too?"

"You are the most infuriating . . ."

"You know something—I'm damned tired of arguing with you." True to his word, he acted, instead. She once again found herself in his arms, but this time she guarded herself against the sensation she knew his kiss could ignite. So, remaining coolly clinical, she let herself enjoy his technique. When his tongue slipped into her mouth, she welcomed the intrusion and relished the taste of it. At the same time, she inhaled the smell of the cologne that permeated his clothes, skin and hair. Then, merely to satisfy an impulse and a fantasy, she reached to stroke the dark hair. Ah, yes, she thought, he would make a fabulous lover . . . he tasted good, he smelled delectable, he knew how to excite a woman expertly. . . .

He took control of her mouth just long enough to ensure that she became breathless, and then he moved the tip of his tongue along the line of her throat very, very slowly. Fire and ice, temptation and satisfaction; his touch promised everything. He kept his hips still, opting, instead, to wedge a leg ever so slightly between her thighs so that she was forced to lean on it until she experienced a stabbing throb. Immediately she pulled back, suppressing the thrill. She also stifled the shiver that his tongue was evoking at the base of her neck. That's quite enough, she thought, but his voice was enticing her, too, whispering, confessing his weaknesses, praising her loveliness. She leaned away, trying to avoid his mouth, but all she managed to do was bury her face in the downy dusk of his hair. The satiny strands clung to her lips and then slid inside, tickling and tantalizing. Even the texture of his hair was exquisite. "Jeff, don't."

He answered by gripping her hand and placing it against his body, holding her fingers captive there until they convulsed, curving along his groin. Dazed, she held him for an instant, his heat scalding her palm— and then she tore her hand away. "Jeff, no . . ."

A polite cough brought the erotic battle to a swift end. Marion Fairmont, their hostess, was standing just inside the doorway. She calmly walked to a side table and turned on a crystal lamp. Then, as if failing to see the raw emotions gripping the pair, she smiled first at Monica and then at Jeff. "The servants must have forgotten to turn on the lights in this room," Marion Fairmont said in a perfectly normal tone. She went to a matching lamp on the other side of the room and turned that one on, too. "There, that's much better, don't you agree?"

Monica had fallen numbly into a deep armchair. Jeff was leaning against the mantelpiece, staring into the flames. Marion Fairmont waited a beat or two longer. "Oh, Jeff, I thought you'd want to know that Mac-Laine Downes is looking for you. I believe he has some important information."

Monica knew the name, and the knowledge did nothing to ease her acute embarrassment. MacLaine Downes was an aged, highly regarded former state governor whose expertise was greatly valued by the present administration. He held many advisory positions, including that of special liaison to the White House concerning various educational projects. For all intents and purposes, because of his regard for youth programs, he was Monica's "boss." He was also an old and cherished friend of the Lewis family and had known Monica since birth.

Meanwhile, Jeff was trying to clear the sensual glaze from his eyes. "Where is he?"

"Outside. Shall I bring him in?"

"Yes, please, Marion."

Monica tried to rise to her feet, but she simply couldn't. This was the perfect time to make an escape, but her legs felt as weak as her head and refused to follow commands. Marion—and, obviously, Jeff, too —knew of Monica's association with MacLaine Downes, so they naturally expected her to stay where she was. The hostess left the room, but returned only moments later with the politician in tow. "I searched until I found him," Marion told MacLaine Downes, nodding toward Jeff. "Oh, and of course you know Judge Lewis's lovely daughter."

The elder statesman smiled in recognition and then bowed his head like a true gentleman. "How are you, my dear Monica? You know," he said, chuckling, "I always feel a slight surprise every time I see you."

"Why is that, Governor?"

"Because I never thought 'Somber' Judge Lewis capable of siring such a beautiful child."

Sensing that Monica was still in a slightly confused state of mind, Marion Fairmont decided to respond for her with a light laugh that was the very model of tact and airy humor. "Oh, Monica comes from a long line of beautiful ladies, so maybe that's the answer."

"It must be," MacLaine Downes laughed, his eyes twinkling. "Anyway, you brighten this rather humid Washington evening, Monica."

Monica was regaining her senses. She thought quickly: it was quite possible that MacLaine Downes might hold the key to her acceptance by Sacramento, since he wielded tremendous clout in all branches of government, coast to coast. One good word from him would probably assure her the new job. But she loathed asking for favors, and this was hardly the time and place to bring up that particular subject. Certainly not with Jeff glowering in the background, anyway. So instead, Monica resorted to acceptable social banter. "You're flattering me outrageously, Governor, but thank you so much, anyhow."

But it was Jeff, in a hushed but clear voice, who cut into the conversation at this point. "MacLaine, do you know that Monica has decided to abandon Washington in hopes of a career in California?"

"Oh, but that's impossible!" Marion Fairmont protested before MacLaine Downes could gather his usually sharp wits and reply to Jeff's oddly timed remark. "I thought that, after tonight, you might decide to take your place as one of Washington's lovely socialites and attend all my parties, Monica." The woman was genuinely disappointed; more than that, she was also quite annoyed that she had not gotten wind of the story before tonight. "Where were you thinking of going, my dear? Not that I will allow it, you understand, but I assume that you were considering San Francisco. Really, Monica, it's the only culturally civilized place in California, you know!"

Monica smiled on hearing that particular myth stated with such blind, uninformed conviction. "The very sophisticated natives of Los Angeles might not agree with you, and neither would the residents of some of California's other cities, but actually, Marion, I would be going to live in Sacramento."

"Sacramento?" Marion Fairmont was aghast. "Los Angeles might be considered an *outré* but still possible alternative to San Francisco, but Sacramento . . . ? Why there, for heaven's sake?"

"If my application is accepted, it would be to head my own department in a special field of education for young people."

MacLaine Downes finally decided to intervene.

Knowing Marion Fairmont only too well, he didn't want to risk a long discussion on that old chestnut of the east coast versus the west coast. Also, Jeff Mac-Kennon, after his initial outburst, had not uttered another word—and Monica was assiduously avoiding that young man's eyes. Oh, yes, there was definite tension in this room. Anyway, Downes had just remembered something. "Come to think of it, my dear Monica, a memo did reach my desk concerning a possible reference from me relating to a job application in your name. I didn't think it was of immediate importance," he continued, "or you or your father would have mentioned it, no doubt." He shrugged and smiled with complacency. "Just a whim or a far-reaching interest for a future possibility, isn't that so? Anyway, I'm sure your father would prefer to keep you under his protective eye—"

"On the contrary," Monica said, interrupting, "my father thinks that starting fresh in California would be wonderful for me."

"Oh, well, my dear, I just assumed . . . I mean . . . after that sad, sad event in your life . . ."

MacLaine Downes instantly realized that he had said something wrong, especially after catching the look of disapproval in Marion's glance. Jeff Mac-Kennon seemed to come to life too, suddenly and surprisingly, and the young man was now staring at Monica with the oddest mixture of emotions crossing his face. *Oh, my Lord,* MacLaine Downes swore, thankful that he had never permitted himself to become enmeshed in emotional or personal relationships. Politics and government were his only passions and he had deliberately never married because he yearned for no other loves. He fervently hoped that Jeff MacKennon would follow his example—because that young man had the makings of a brilliant career in politics.

But the suave politician recovered his usual poise, and he recouped his losses by employing a time-honored political maneuver: he merely changed the subject. "Well, my dear Monica, you and your father must really join me for dinner sometime in the near future. We can relax and then we can talk about your plans and your dreams."

Monica knew that her "plans and dreams" had been urbanely but politely dismissed from MacLaine Downes's busy schedule. However, she remembered her manners and played the game to perfection. "That would be delightful, Governor, thank you. Yes, Father and I would very much like to have dinner with you . . . sometime."

Now MacLaine Downes was free to cut short the small talk and get directly to his original reason for searching out Jeff MacKennon. "A contingent from the White House has just arrived here." He raised an eyebrow when Jeff didn't answer. "Jeff, I think you should know that they're all key members of the President's staff."

"Yes, of course," Jeff murmured, snapping out of his trance with a visible effort. "Thank you for letting me know, MacLaine. I'll be there in a moment."

"Don't be long." The elder statesman thought it

wise to make that suggestion, sending Jeff a hidden warning concerning Monica. "After all, the administration's top men are waiting to see you."

"I promise, I'll be right there."

After MacLaine Downes and their hostess had left the library, Monica and Jeff finally stared at each other. "I'll make it easier for you, Jeff—I'm leaving now."

"Please stay."

"Why? Since I don't want to see you torn between staying with me out of politeness and talking to the President's men to advance your career, I won't detain you any longer."

He was clearly shaken. "I want to stay here with you, and it has nothing to do with being polite. Please wait for me. I won't be long . . . talking to the White House staff, I mean, and then—"

"No." She had finally managed to extricate herself from the armchair. "Take your time, because I won't be here."

"Listen to me," he pleaded. "We have to talk."

"I don't think so." She reached the doorway. "The only talking you really want to do is with people who will help your career. Listen," she insisted, shaking her head, "I don't blame you. I understand: You've been bitten by the political bug and you're suffering from the same incurable disease that's gotten into almost everybody's system in this damned town. It's called the 'I'll-get-to-the-top-or-I'll-die syndrome.' Well, I don't have that particular bug. All I want is to go on with *my* career—unimportant as that might seem to everybody else."

"That's a bit harsh, don't you think?"

"Oh, really? Well, let's just say I've received some very uninspiring reactions from everybody, okay? Governor Downes laughingly supposes that I applied for the job in California on a girlish whim, Marion thinks I should spend the rest of my life giggling and flirting on the social circuit, my friends react as if I were about to embark on a loony mission of mercy among lepers on the western frontier, and my father, because of his own misplaced feelings of guilt, is merely indulging me." Her voice took on an icy edge. "And as for *you*—"

"Now, just hold it a second." He went to the door and leaned against it, blocking her way. "Don't start to fling accusations at me before hearing me out."

"I've heard what you have to 'say,' Jeff, and I get the message, loud and clear."

"Is that the only message you've gotten from me?"

"You're damned right! And if I ever thought that the main reason you urged me to stay was so that I could find a real challenge and pursue the practice of law for my own intellectual satisfaction, that macho scene you just pulled on me sure changed my mind."

"I wasn't handing you a line when I told you to stay and build a successful law practice here in Washington —I still feel that way," he emphasized sharply. "However, that doesn't have anything to do with the fact that you excite me. I get real pleasure from touching you and having you touch me—and I want more of it. Also, I don't think that it's a crime to feel good about another human."

"What's that supposed to mean?"

"I've been waiting for you to deny that you feel the same way . . . to deny that you've ever responded to me."

"I can't deny it," she said bluntly, "but I think I've been honest with you."

"I know," he murmured. "Your excuse is that you don't want any entanglements in your life."

"It's not just an excuse." Maybe she was being a fool, but he had pushed her beyond caution. "Listen, I know you think my life has been pretty darned cushy up until now—coming from a rich family, always protected, spoiled rotten, a brat and a maverick—"

"Monica, stop it."

But once she had begun, she couldn't stop. "But I've also been dealt a good dose of misery in my life. Okay, since I'm a hopeless noncomformist I couldn't react the way everybody expected me to act—wasting my time feeling sorry for myself, moaning and wringing my hands. I have this stubborn streak of independence which wouldn't allow me to act like a ninny and beg for sympathy. Instead, I went and found myself a meaningful job which I grew to love. I never want to look back at the past, but more than anything else, Jeff MacKennon, I don't want you to come barging into my life, making a mess of things."

"Because?" he urged softly and cautiously.

"Because in spite of all my brave words, I love it when you hold me and touch me and want me. And the last thing I need right now is to get involved with you!"

A clock was fretfully ticking somewhere in the room, and in another part of the town house, the White

House staff members were waiting. But Jeff seemed mindless of that fact and he remained where he was with his back against the door. "Thanks for spelling out how you feel about me," he whispered. "It might be hard for you to believe this, but I needed to hear it, badly." There was a seriousness about him now which was slightly frightening. "All right, I've listened to your declaration of independence, and you've finally convinced me that you need freedom and space. But now . . . I want you to do me a favor, Monica."

"What favor?"

"I want you to come here to me."

No, don't go near him, was her first reaction. But then she caught sight of the growing seriousness that gave his face an expression of breathtaking gentleness . . . and her fear faded. He slowly lifted his hands, as if to urge her to take them, and the gesture was unthreatening. She took one step and then another, and then she went to him and felt his arms fold around her. There was nothing possessive or demanding in his embrace; instead, he held her with all the comfort and compassion she so desperately needed at the moment. If he had been rough or sensual or selfish, she would have torn herself away and left him, but he just continued to hold her with a mesmerizing tenderness. His whisper was gentle, too. "If you go to California and find you've made a big mistake, if you're terribly unhappy, what would you do then?"

"Admit that I made a mistake and go on to something else, I suppose." She leaned against him, drained, limp. "But I'll never know until I try, will I?"

"No," he whispered, stroking her hair almost lovingly, "because you're a hopeless brat and an incorrigible maverick." He felt her smile as she pressed her face against his chest. "And what about us?"

"*If* I go and then *if* I come back like a penitent puppy, I'll call you, ask you out to dinner, and we'll take it from there."

"And . . . if you don't come back?"

"We'll survive, Jeff. We're both very strong people."

"That's somewhat cynical, don't you think?"

She suddenly thought of Cissy and shuddered a little. If anything, the thought served to strengthen her resolve to make the break quietly and swiftly. "No, it's just common sense talking, that's all." But how would she feel tomorrow . . . and after tomorrow? Better not to dwell on that. "Jeff, I've kept you from those officials long enough."

"It's all right, don't leave me," he entreated.

"I'll have to, sooner or later." She pushed herself away from him. "I'll go through the terrace."

"Wait." He caught her arm again gently. "How did you get to this party?"

"I came with Cissy in her car, but she left with somebody. . . ." She was glad to talk about mundane things because her heart was doing funny acrobatics against her ribs. "I'll take a cab—no, don't protest. I'll call you to let you know what happens with the job, one way or the other, okay?"

"Okay." He seemed strangely quiet, as if he had wrestled with a problem and had finally found the only solution. "Monica?"

"Yes?"

"Call me from California, anytime and for any reason, all right?"

"I promise. Good-bye."

"Monica . . ."

"Good-bye."

Without looking back, Monica walked out of the room. She wound her way through the terrace and across the garden, behaving quite normally as she moved through the crowd of guests. She even stopped now and then to say a word or two. Finally, she ignored the question in Marion Fairmont's eyes and kissed her cheek and said a polite good night. As she left the elegant party where she had expected to have so much fun, she realized that, on the contrary, she had probably spent one of the most miserable nights of her life. One thing she swore, however: Jeff must never know what it had cost her to leave him.

Only five days after Marion Fairmont's party, Monica received a phone call from Sacramento. She had been accepted to head the Youth Advancement Agency for the Department of Education there. After weeks of nerve-racking waiting, her future was resolved. She wavered about whether or not to call MacLaine Downes—since she had been told that it had been on his very strong recommendation that she had been hired—to find out why he had suddenly changed his mind and acted so swiftly on her behalf. But instead of phoning and perhaps embarrassing him, she opted to write him a warm letter thanking him from the bottom of her heart. As for Jeff, mercifully, she hadn't heard a word from him. Just as well, she thought; she would call him once she was settled in California. By then, with thousands of miles between them, she could come to grips with the terrible realization that she had left Washington already halfway in love with him.

3

After six months in Sacramento, Monica finally felt settled and comfortable. She heard from Jeff once in a while—a few words scribbled on an official memo or a brief inquiry as to how she was doing when exchanging phone calls concerning youth-education business —but nothing more personal. So be it, she told herself, determined to relegate Jeff MacKennon to the back of her mind. And yet she often found herself remembering the things about him that fascinated her, and then she would be angry with herself. The entire episode with Jeff MacKennon was very bewildering . . . and she couldn't explain it away.

Once, on a television newscast, she caught a fast glimpse of his face at a White House function and, deliberately dispassionate, she still had to admit that

Jeff MacKennon was the most attractive man she had ever known. The cameras had concentrated on the President, of course, but still the lights had caught Jeff's raven-black hair and dusky eyes, doing marvelous things to both, and she was left feeling foolishly empty and sad and alone. She shook off the feeling of sadness soon enough, because many new things occupied her mind now. But her reaction to a mere glimpse of him on television had really shaken and scared her for a time.

Her new work in Sacramento was thoroughly enjoyable. She found her work challenging and she had made a host of new friends. Holly Winston, Monica's administrative assistant, was bright and friendly and close to Monica's own age; the two soon became friends. One night, sitting in front of the fire at Monica's apartment while they drank wine and listened to music, Holly, apparently in all innocence, said, "Monica, you need some male companionship!"

Monica looked up, surprised. "Did you just dream up that idea, or have you been pondering the problem for a while?"

"Just thought of it, really," Holly said, undaunted by Monica's friendly sarcasm. "I'm quite serious, you know. You need male attention."

Monica poured more wine into their glasses. "Okay, I'll bite. Why?"

"Because it's about time in the natural course of human events, that's why."

"Stop trying to look like an oracle, Holly, it really doesn't become you." Monica rolled her eyes in a

gesture of mock martyrdom. "But I'm listening—
although I'll probably live to regret it."

"Well, I was looking around this place and I suddenly thought that since it's almost finished . . ."

"Not *quite* finished. I still have some odds and ends
to buy."

"But still," Holly persisted, "you're doing such a
fantastic job getting all the new programs on track at
the Youth Advancement Agency, and you've practically become a happy native of Sacramento in just six
months, so . . ."

"So?"

"I think you should relax now and start enjoying
something very important in the life of an attractive,
intelligent, normal woman."

"Such as . . . ?"

"Such as romance, for instance," Holly declared.

"Oh, I see," she laughed. "Romance! Just like
that?"

"With an interesting male specimen, of course."

Monica settled back, amused. "And where do you
suggest I find this paragon of lovers?"

"A woman like you should have no problem finding
a willing victim," Holly stated, raising her glass in a
toast to Monica's good looks.

"I haven't the time or inclination to go beating the
bushes for a lover, so forget it." But Monica thought
Holly deserved a little teasing, anyway. "Of course, if
you're really concerned about my celibate state, you
could be a good sport and prove yourself a genuine
friend by lending me your Gavin for a night or two."

Holly Winston and Gavin Spencer were a classic

pair, solidly in love, and a sure bet to spend the rest of their lives together. Right now, they were sharing a small apartment while diligently building careers—Holly in education and Gavin in the news media—and saving their money for the future. They were headed for marriage, a white picket fence and a bunch of babies, and they seemed gloriously joyous about the prospect of growing old and senile together. Knowing this, Monica playfully dared to suggest such a fantastic idea. Holly waited with dramatic flair before retorting, "Purr at Gavin even once, and I'll scratch your eyes out, Monica Lewis! Go find your own man!"

"So much for true friendship," Monica sighed, and then laughed. "All kidding aside, thanks for being concerned about me, Holly, but as for romance, I'm just not interested at the moment. Sorry."

Holly leaned back against a pile of Japanese pillows and gazed at Monica through narrowed lids. "You've been burned recently and you're still hurting, huh?"

"No, that's not the way it is at all," Monica murmured, turning to stare into the small grate of the fireplace. "I just don't want to become emotional about anything or anyone for a while."

"What was he, a lousy lover—or maybe *too* good?"

"I told you, it was nothing of the kind."

"A husband, then?"

Monica smiled, but there was little humor in it. "I was married, once, but that was long ago. It didn't end nicely." She did some soul-searching for a moment. "I haven't thought about my husband—his name was Jim, by the way—for a while, and truthfully, that episode in my life has little to do with my resolve not to become involved with anybody." She leaned forward and hugged her knees. "I'm only sorry we didn't have any children," she added, as if she were talking to herself, "and, maybe subconsciously, that's why I enjoy working with young people so much."

"There's plenty of time ahead for the patter of little feet, for both of us," Holly interjected, deliberately keeping the flow of conversation light and easy. How interesting that Monica had been married and had never mentioned the fact! Oh, well, Holly reasoned, everybody had secrets.

The disc on the stereo finished playing and the machine shut itself off. The room was very quiet. Monica knew she had reopened an old wound thinking of Jim, a wound that had been quietly healing until Jeff MacKennon walked into her life, a wound that had become painful again because of an irrational yearning and longing for Jeff MacKennon. And it wasn't only a distracted physical wanting; it was something more basic, deeper, dangerous. . . .

"Hey, Monica, are you still with me?"

After a mental shake, Monica spoke. "Sorry."

"Everything okay?"

"Sure, I'm fine."

But Holly wasn't fooled. "You look spooked." She eyed her friend quite critically and then came to a decision. "You haven't had anything to eat, so why don't you come along and have dinner with Gavin and me? I'm supposed to pick him up at the studio in half an hour."

"No, I'm not hungry, but thanks anyway."

"Join us just for a drink, then."

"No, Holly, I'd rather . . . I mean, I planned to do some things around the apartment." She had almost blurted the truth, that she preferred to be alone at the moment. "We'll get together for dinner some other time, all right?"

"Okay," Holly said, giving in to Monica's mood. "I'll see you in the office tomorrow morning, then." She got her purse and headed for the door, but she stopped just long enough to assure herself that her friend was really going to be all right alone. Grudgingly satisfied, she waved. "Good-bye."

Monica answered with a reassuring smile. "And give my love to Gavin."

Finally alone, Monica sat for a while, her mind blissfully blank. But it wasn't long before the images began to attack her again, and she shrugged them aside. She put another record on the stereo, concentrating on the music. But that ruse didn't work; neither did another glass of wine help very much. All right, she told herself, don't fight it anymore! Think it out, before you go crazy.

Without a doubt, her move to Sacramento had been a boon to her career. She had been encouraged to create new programs and she felt that she had more than met expectations by planning dynamic youth educational projects. She was very happy with her working conditions and with the people concerned. As for her social life, she couldn't really ask for anything better—or less of a hassle. She had made new friends and there was no scarcity of casual companionship. She enjoyed the full spectrum of living in the west— from skiing weekends in the Sierra Nevada to concerts, operas, and museums in San Francisco, to boating and swimming in the marinas and bays and beaches of the Pacific. And if she needed close, confidential support, she knew that she could always count on Holly and Gavin to come to her aid with all the resources of true friendship. So—where was the hitch? Was she really so unsatisfied, so alone amidst people, because Jeff MacKennon was far, far away?

Yes, obviously, and it was useless to lie to herself. Suddenly truly exasperated, she wrestled with the knowledge that she had woven a neat trap. She couldn't stop thinking about Jeff. How ironic! No emotional entanglements, huh? Perhaps it would have been better if she *had* slept with him! Well, it really didn't help to let her imagination run amok. The best course she could follow now was to rid herself of the MacKennon Malady by finding a good antidote. It was alien to her character to mope around, longing for the impossible. She knew that she was sufficiently balanced and mature enough to combat any obstacle. What's more, she really didn't have any choice in the matter, right? And she had the perfect antidote right at her fingertips, namely, her work.

Monica could sense trouble the moment she entered the office and caught a glimpse of Holly's face. "What's the matter?"

"There's a report on your desk," Holly said, "which I don't think you're going to like."

"What does it say?"

"You'd better read it for yourself."

The report was heavy. Monica balanced it in her

hands for a moment before opening it. Ever since that evening with Holly when she had resolved to throw herself into her work like a fiend to ward off unwanted thoughts of Jeff MacKennon, Monica had put all her energy into a special work-pay program for students interested in community and government service careers. It was a far-reaching plan, one which would ensure that a steady stream of good minds continued to flow from the high schools into all branches of local, state and federal government. She was pleased and happy with it, knowing she had applied all her training to something meaningful, but she also knew that there were built-in pitfalls—primarily, the costs. However, optimistically she had submitted a comprehensive summary of her program for evaluation by the committee.

Now, with Holly hovering nervously in the background, Monica opened the report and read the findings of the state budget committee: The committee regretted to inform Ms. Monica Lewis, director of the Youth Advancement Agency, that, due to forced budget cuts, they had "redirected" the funds originally allocated for her work-pay program. Attached, also, were letters and memos from a number of assemblymen and state senators who expressed their regrets because they'd had high hopes for Monica's enlightened new youth programs. However, the expansion of a summer internship program for gifted students would have to be shelved for this fiscal year. Hopefully, something could be set up for next year; meanwhile, *sorry,* Ms. Lewis.

It was far worse than Monica had expected. "I was

hoping that I'd get at least *some* of the program funding," she murmured. "Oh, Holly, this is awful!"

"Don't let it get you down, Monica." Holly's pretty face broke into a valiant smile. "Okay, so there won't be any funding for a year, but the report, without exception, says that everybody thinks the program is worthwhile. So you've had a momentary setback, that's all. Next year the program will take off, you'll see!"

Monica wasn't convinced. "I've put a large hunk of my life into this project. . . ."

"What's a life worth in government?" Holly laughed, but it was sympathetic. "Come on, be realistic. It'll take time, but your program *will* succeed, Monica."

"I suppose you're right—sometimes I'm too impatient. Still, it hurts."

"I know, but there's nothing you can do about it right now," Holly said practically. "Look, you've been working like a dog on this program and you're tired and beat. Why don't you treat yourself to just one night of relaxation—instead of working late—and come and have dinner with Gavin and me. You promised you would, but you keep making excuses." Holly added an extra bit of inducement. "We'll go to that Mexican restaurant you like so much, okay? Please?"

Monica suddenly felt flat and defeated. "Okay, and thanks for caring so much, Holly."

Although Monica tried hard to be sociably cheery, dinner that evening with Holly and Gavin was strictly downbeat. Gavin had been a few minutes late, so he found the two women already seated at a table when he arrived. One look at Monica's face was enough to tell him that something was wrong. However, after a fast glance at Holly, he wisely decided to keep his mouth shut until information voluntarily came his way.

The waiter took their order and then a heavy silence fell on the trio. Finally Monica glanced at the pair, and the sight did nothing to help her sense of depression. They were so happy . . . and she felt so miserable; they were together, and she was very, very alone. Monica fought the stupid, self-serving tightness that strangled her throat, and she breathed a very hefty sigh of relief when the waiter returned with their food.

After a while, Gavin's air of polite unconcern completely deserted him. "Oh, for God's sake, what's the matter with you two? Holly, you haven't muttered a word to me so far—and you, Monica, could depress a hyena!" He glared from Monica to her plate and then back at her. "Stop pushing that olive around your plate and put it, instead, in your mouth where it belongs. You haven't eaten anything, and your tacos are getting all soggy."

It was true; her plate was a jumble of untasted food. In the background, doleful Mexican folk songs— mostly inspired by unrequited love—only added to the gloom. Monica put her fork on the table and picked up one of the soggy tacos. With effort, she took a bite out of the shell. "See, I'm eating."

"What's bugging you, Monica?"

The taco completely disintegrated in her hands. She put the pieces back on her plate and gave up the charade of trying to eat. "I was informed by the budget committee today that some of my funds have been 'redirected' to another agency. Gavin, I'm so furious!''

Holly clutched at Gavin's arm as if seeking reassurance. "I told her to take it easy. She shouldn't take it personally, for goodness' sake."

"Holly's right," Gavin agreed, and then he planted a kiss on Holly's cheek to confirm his belief in her common sense. "Look, Monica, that's the best advice —don't take it as a personal put-down."

"I don't," she insisted, "but I'm very disappointed. I've worked so hard, and so has Holly, and I don't want to wait another year to get the work-pay program in gear. The project's too important to be dumped for lack of funds!"

"It's rough, I know," Gavin said, "but those are the facts of life in government, Monica. There's nothing you can do but wait until next year."

"I won't wait," she said emphatically.

"Have you any other ideas?" Holly asked, surprised but a little hopeful, too. She, of all people, knew the extent of the time and energy Monica had lavished on the project. What she didn't suspect was the underlying reason why Monica had half-killed herself refining this particular one. "Did you just think of something?"

"It's a very vague idea, that's all." Monica nodded, irritated with herself for contemplating the possibility of such a solution. But then she glanced at Holly's face and immediately felt rotten about building up her friend's hopes on the basis of a foolish idea. "But it won't work, so forget about it, Holly."

At this point, Gavin was willing to clutch at any straw if it would bring a smile back to Holly's face. "What is it? Tell us, at least!"

"Come on, Monica, please?" echoed Holly.

Monica frowned. "I was an idiot for mentioning it, but now that I've put my foot in my mouth, I'll level with you—and then we'll try to find *another* solution." She stopped to take a deep breath. "I thought if I could interest somebody in Washington in our problem . . ."

"Washington?" Holly was puzzled, but only for a split second. "Of course, that's a great idea! You lived and worked in Washington and I'm sure you've made plenty of contacts. You probably know everybody in the top ranks at the Department of Education, don't you?"

"Yes, most of them."

"Then contact them," Gavin piped in, "and tell them your story about the budget cuts, and lean on them a little to see if they can help you."

"That's the problem," Monica murmured. "I can't do that."

"Why not?" Holly cried.

"Because I don't like asking favors from anybody."

Holly and Gavin exchanged bewildered looks. "Come on, Monica," Gavin coaxed, "be sensible. There's nothing shady or immoral or illegal in asking for help for your project, for God's sake! It's done all the time and it's a time-honored procedure in government."

Monica stopped him right there. "Oh, don't I know it! I grew up surrounded by people who took advantage of that 'time-honored procedure' all the time. I'm a product of Washington's inner circle, remember? I swore I would never stoop to such methods." She realized she probably sounded a bit rigid and pompous. "Listen, my father drummed a great deal of idealistic theory into my head, and I guess I still believe in it. That's why I came to Sacramento—to stand on my own two feet and not be indebted, professionally or personally, to *anybody*."

Holly saw her opening and she got a solid point across to Monica. "Okay, I'll buy that, but I think you're arguing apples and oranges. Nobody's asking you to compromise yourself for your *own* gain, either professional or personal. You're not asking for anything for yourself, are you? You're fighting to preserve a very meaningful program for some very deserving youngsters, remember?"

"Yes, I know. . . ."

Holly saw Monica waver, so she kept hammering away. "I thought you were *furious* about having the program put on the back burner."

"I am," Monica insisted.

"Then, since you've thought of a wonderful alternative, one that's strictly legal and feasible, why are you fighting it so hard?"

"Because . . ." Monica would have to admit that the person who would have to be contacted, as director of program funding of the Department of Education in Washington, was Jeff MacKennon—and she just couldn't do it. Your emotions have really gotten you into a beautiful mess this time, Monica Lewis! she seethed. Jeff had urged her to call if she

CAPITOL AFFAIR

needed help; the only sane and practical solution was
easily at hand, and she was hesitating because she
dreaded, on a personal level, to open communications
with the very person who could help her save the
program. "I'll have to think this out," she finally
hedged.

But Holly persisted. "Do you happen to know the
chief honcho of the funding office?"

"Yes, I know him."

"Then please, Monica, if you've had past dealings
with him, contact him. Don't be so stubborn," Holly
blurted.

Monica was about to counter with something caus-
tic, but she caught herself in time. Poor Holly and
Gavin. She didn't blame them for being exasperated
by her contradictory attitude. She had to placate
them, at least temporarily. "All right, look, I promise to
think about it very seriously, and I'll let you know what
I decide." She smiled at the pair. "Don't worry, leave
it to me to come up with an answer. Now . . . I think
I've ruined your evening quite enough, so I'll leave
you two alone and wander on home."

They protested at the same time. "No, stay. . . ."

"I want to go home and think." Monica stood. "I'll
see you in the morning, Holly. Good-bye, Gavin."

Monica sat cross-legged on her bed and thought it
out all over again: only six months away from Washington, and she was already asking for favors! So
much for the "declaration of independence" with
which she had bombarded Jeff's ears. Still, Holly had
struck at the truth when she'd stated that the request

72

for funds would be for the good of the student program, not for Monica Lewis's sake. To think otherwise, even for an instant, would not be truly professional. And yet, it was up to her, Monica, to ask him, Jeff, for help. It simply had to be done. For the students. For the program. Because it was the kind of positive, idealistic project which had prompted her move to California in the first place. With a groan and a mumbled curse, she shut off the light and flung herself back on the pillows. She stopped trying to think so that she could sleep, but she felt frazzled and overheated. She stripped off her nightie and lay back, staring at nothing.

The next morning, Monica arrived at the office thirty minutes early because she needed the time alone to prepare herself to call Jeff. First, she made a full pot of strong coffee in the small closet that was used as a pantry. She waited, getting her thoughts together, while the coffee brewed. Then she poured a cup and, taking it to her desk, glanced at her wristwatch. Seven-forty. Holly wouldn't be in for a while yet, and it was ten-forty in Washington. It was a good time to call. Jeff would probably be at his desk. She reached for the phone, hesitated, and then took the plunge. There was a slight pause while Jeff's secretary transferred the call to his private line. Then suddenly he was there. "Monica, nice to hear from you again. How's the wild west?"

Oh, no, she thought; however, the program was at stake, remember? So she answered smoothly, "As beautiful as ever, thanks."

"How are you doing?"

If he only knew! "I'm fine," she dissembled artfully.

"And your work? From the little you've told me and what I've managed to glean through the grapevine, I gather that you're really pushing through a wonderful list of programs."

She had the opening she needed. "Jeff, that's why I'm calling you. One of the programs has suffered a terrible setback."

"What happened?"

"The funds for the work-pay program have been redirected to other agencies. The budget committee's report was optimistic about next year, but the best I can hope for is a maybe. Jeff, believe me, the project is so worthwhile!"

"I know," he assured her emphatically.

"And I'm afraid that if my program has to be abandoned this year, I'll never get a chance to implement it." She hesitated, in order to get her thoughts together and to sound as rational and reasonable as possible. "The last time I saw you, you said I was to call you if I needed anything. Well, that's what I'm doing, Jeff, because I want to know if you can help me obtain funds from your office so that the work-pay program can be put into action this year. Can you help me?" Without waiting for an answer, she added, as clearly as possible, "Although I would appreciate it so very much, I want you to understand that I'm asking this for the young people of this state—and not for myself. Now, what do you think?"

"It's possible," he replied cautiously. This was the public servant speaking, not the friend. Obviously he had decided to use the same businesslike attitude she was utilizing. "I'll review the year's fiscal allocations myself, to cut through some of the bureaucratic red tape, and I'll get back to you soon."

"Thank you." She felt a tremendous relief, but tried to hide it. "That's more than I expected."

"Don't thank me yet, because I can't promise anything. However, I'll do what I can."

"And you will call me soon?"

"Just as soon as I have something concrete to tell you."

Not until she hung up the receiver did she realize how hard her hand was trembling. There—she had done it! It had wrecked her nerves to make that call, she reflected, but immediately chided herself for putting her own feelings on a higher priority than her work. Anyway, she rationalized, other than a few phone calls and a professional debt, her involvement with Jeff MacKennon in this matter would remain, as in the past, negligible.

"Hello, Monica, wake up!" Holly stood there, waving her fingers in front of Monica's staring eyes.

"When did you arrive?"

Holly sighed. "I came in, banged the door shut, said hello, made a racket throwing my purse and briefcase on the desk, and you didn't even blink. Daydreaming on a grand scale?"

"Hardly that," Monica murmured, still trying to calm down. "Please get me another cup of coffee, will you?"

"Sure." Holly fussed with the cups and came right back. "Thinking about the funding, I hope?"

"That, and nothing else, don't worry."

"Well, what did you decide?"

"I decided to bend my stiff neck for the good of the majority," she answered, mixing her metaphors and not really caring at the moment. "I called Washington."

"Good for you! I knew you'd come through once you had a chance to sleep on it."

Monica smothered a smile at the irony of that supposition. "Anyway, if a Jeff MacKennon calls from Washington, please be sure I get the message, okay?"

"You bet. He's the honcho who hands out the big bucks at the Department of Education, isn't he?"

"Yes." She offered no other information. "Let's keep our fingers crossed, Holly."

Three days passed and Monica heard nothing from Jeff. She found herself jumping every time the phone on her desk rang. Holly became more than a little curious about Monica's reactions, and when Gavin stopped by the office, they exchanged quizzical looks. "Anything yet from Washington?" he asked Holly while Monica, busy on another matter, couldn't hear.

"No, nothing yet," Holly informed him. "Gavin . . ."

"Something on your mind?"

"Yes, as a matter of fact. Have you noticed anything peculiar about Monica?"

"What do you mean, peculiar? Sure, she's been acting like a repressed nut case ever since the program's money was taken away, but who can blame her?"

"Well, my thick-headed darling, what I meant was, I

know how much the work-pay project means to her, but every time that darned phone rings and it's not Jeff MacKennon, she looks more than dejected—she looks haunted. Now, I may be wrong, but I'm starting to suspect there's more to this Washington business than Monica's told us. . . ."

When Jeff's call finally came, luck would have it that Monica was not in her office. Holly took the call. "Yes, Mr. MacKennon, I know who you are," she said in her best business voice, "but I'm sorry, Ms. Lewis isn't here at the moment." What a sexy-sounding voice this guy had! "May I take a message?"

"Just ask Ms. Lewis to call back, will you?"

"I certainly will, Mr. MacKennon."

Holly could hardly wait for Monica's return, and as soon as the door opened she practically jumped out of her chair. "Guess what?"

With an unusual snap in her words, Monica replied, "Don't play games with me, Holly. What is it?"

Holly was too excited to notice the lapse. "Jeff MacKennon called half an hour ago. He wants you to call him back."

"Thank you . . . and, Holly, I'm sorry I snapped at you."

"Never mind, just call him back!"

Monica tried to be calm. She reached for the phone and dialed. After a few extension switches, she heard Jeff speak. "Monica, I have wonderful news. My office might be able to provide funding for your program for one year."

"Jeff!" Monica was thrilled. "That's terrific!"

"It's not certain yet, of course, but I believe it may even be possible to release the money in time for summer implementation, if I pull a lot of strings and keep the red tape to a minimum."

"Can you?"

"I'll give it my best, Monica. Meanwhile, I'm sending someone from my office to visit you and gather information on your project, okay? I'm afraid that's necessary before final approval can be granted by our committee."

"Oh, yes, of course. I promise to have all the paperwork in order and a complete report ready so that there won't be any delay."

"Then that's about it. Perhaps I shouldn't stick my neck out, but I think your chances are good. And, Monica . . ." His voice softened, became warmer. "I'm glad you remembered me when you needed help."

"Jeff . . ." She would spoil everything if she told him how reluctant she had been to call him—and why. So she kept her words warm but impersonal. "Thanks for everything you've done, and I'll be waiting to meet your representative. Keep in touch, won't you?"

"Of course I will."

He *had* been glad to help her, she realized after she put the receiver down. The thought made her smile; however, she had completely forgotten about Holly. "I gather your Mr. MacKennon is getting some action on the funding, am I right?"

"Yes, isn't that wonderful? Oh, Holly, we may not have to wait until next year, after all."

"Great!" she said with heartfelt enthusiasm. However, at the moment Holly was more interested in something else. "This Jeff MacKennon-with-the-sexy-voice, how well do you know him, hm-m-m?"

Monica kept her cool and nothing showed in her face. "I know him quite well, in an official capacity, my friend." But she relented a bit, immediately. "However, it's true that he's a very sexy man. *Now,* shall we get to work on our report so that Mr. MacKennon's representative will find everything in perfect order?"

"Sure," Holly agreed, instinctively knowing that Monica was hiding something, but also wise enough to realize that the truth would eventually surface. "Sure. . . ."

For the next few days they worked until they were bone-weary, but Monica and Holly put together a solid program report in record time. Once finished, the report was placed within arm's reach on Monica's desk, next to a small vase filled daily with fresh flowers. As she worked, she found herself gazing apprehensively at it. Was it too concise, or too detailed? No, she decided for the dozenth time, it was just fine. Still, she put her hand out and tapped the manila folder again, as if to reassure herself one more time. Yes, it was perfect the way it was.

Holly's mind was equally preoccupied with the importance of the report's contents. She knew that if Monica could pull off the miracle of finding funds through Jeff MacKennon's office, it would be the coup of all time. Seeking to reassure herself, too, Holly touched the folder, but when she saw Monica frown, she let her hands fuss with the bunch of irises in the small vase. "Holly, don't worry," Monica murmured.

"I can't help it."

"We've done everything possible. Now all we can do is wait and see if Jeff's office comes through with the money. Stop fretting."

"I can't—and you're not fooling me with your queen-of-the-ice act, either!"

Monica put her work aside, sighing. "Okay, so I *am* worried, but we're not going to get any work done in this office if we worry ourselves into a tizzy about it, are we?"

"No, I guess not."

"So let's try to concentrate on our work until we know for sure, all right?"

Holly put on a happy face. "Okay."

"For starters, why don't we refile all those financial reports we've been poring over for hours and hours?" She pointed to a pile of papers stacked high against the wall. "Hopefully, all our toil will not have been in vain," she said wryly.

Holly nodded and lifted an armful of papers off the floor. "Do you want to go out to lunch, Monica? I could sure go for a slice of pizza, with *all* the fixings!"

Monica reached into the desk's bottom drawer and pulled out a brown paper bag. "Sorry, but here's my lunch."

Holly looked dubious. "What did you bring?"

"Peanut butter, honey and sprouts on whole-wheat bread."

"Ugh, how awful!"

"But nutritious," Monica countered with mock seriousness.

"So's pizza, when you think of it! Aw, come on,"

Holly prodded, "let's go out to lunch and eat up a storm of calories."

"Honestly, I can't. I promised some of the kids in the program that I would make the rounds of the offices where they're working and pay them a lunch-time visit. They'd be disappointed if I didn't show, Holly."

Holly gave up the struggle and resigned herself to filing the stack of financial reports. Monica could hear her slamming the steel drawers of the filing cabinets in the crammed storage area that also served as the office's only entryway. Monica went back to her own work. Suddenly she heard Holly talking to somebody. Gavin, maybe? Just then, the door flew open and Holly, looking a bit shaken, came into the office. "Monica . . ."

"What is it?" Thinking that something awful had happened to her friend, Monica got up and rushed around the desk. "What's the matter with you?"

"Jeff MacKennon is here."

Monica couldn't help smiling; Holly could be so foggy at times! "You mean the fiscal representative *from* Jeff's office is here, don't you?"

"No, I mean . . ."

Monica wasn't paying too much attention to what Holly was frantically trying to explain. "Jeff certainly sent somebody quickly, didn't he? That's great! Well, ask the man to come in."

"You're the one who doesn't understand," Holly blurted, exasperated. "I'm trying to tell you that Jeff MacKennon—all six gorgeous feet of him—is *here!*"

Jeff walked into the small office just then. Monica

could only stare. Suddenly she felt elated; she also felt devastated. All she could think of saying was, "What are you doing in Sacramento, for God's sake?"

"I'm here to study the report for your funding, of course," he replied, totally at ease.

"But why *you?*"

"That's easily explained," he assured her, stepping closer as though to kiss her hello. When she backed away, he merely smiled. "But to tell you the truth, I was expecting a warmer welcome."

Holly, gaping at Jeff, seemed a blur to Monica; all she could focus on was Jeff's face. "Why?"

"Because I'm an eternal optimist," he confessed disarmingly. "Haven't you discovered that yet?" He saw Monica's eyes flash toward the pretty woman standing behind him, and he sensitively changed his tactics. "Seriously, my calendar was clear for a few days and I thought I would personally handle your case so that, with luck, I can accelerate the decision on the funding for your project."

She believed only half his story. Hers was a tiny agency, and the amount of money she needed was small potatoes compared to the grants issued to other, larger programs throughout the nation. She was sure that Jeff MacKennon didn't make a habit of personally investigating every petition that reached his office. After all, he was the director of program funding for the Department of Education—not some errand boy! No, he was here for a very specific reason, most likely to do some grass-roots politicking which he could eventually use for his own benefit. That he might have come to Sacramento mainly to see *her* was a possibility that she viewed with caution; perhaps, to serve his overly inflated ego, he had come to see for himself if she were thoroughly miserable and yet too proud to admit her mistake! "I'm not ungrateful, Jeff, but I just assumed you would send some minor official, that's all."

"That would be too cold, too impersonal," he said. "After all, what are close friends for?"

When he was in this sort of mood, she knew that he was impossible and unpredictable. Uppermost in her mind, however, was a very basic set of facts: she had asked for the funding; she needed the money desperately; he knew how badly she wanted the grant. So, since she had placed herself in the position of approaching him with begging bowl in hand, what else could she do but play along with him? "I'm surprised anyway."

Just then, Holly found her tongue. "I'm surprised too, especially since I never thought I'd get the chance to meet you. Mr. MacKennon, I'm glad you came because Monica's program is worth saving." She even dared to imply, "I'm sure you'll feel the same way once you've read our report."

Monica remembered her manners. "Jeff, I'd like you to meet my assistant, Holly Winston."

He gave Holly one of his super smiles. "I happen to agree with you, Holly, even from the little I know about the program. That's why I'm here personally in Sacramento."

Monica decided that the least she could do was give him the benefit of the doubt. For the good of the program, she told herself. Meanwhile, she had to put a stop to Holly's drooling; her friend appeared ready to ravish him right on the spot! "Weren't you just about ready to go to lunch, Holly?"

Her friend quickly got the hint, and she made a great show of looking at her wristwatch. "Oh, yes, it's getting late, isn't it? Well, I'll see you later, Monica, and I'm sure I'll see you too, Mr. MacKennon."

"Yes," he said, "I'll be around for a day or two. Have a nice lunch."

"Thanks," Holly replied with a brilliant smile and an airy wave, "and good-bye."

They were alone. "All right," Monica said in her most direct, no-nonsense voice, "suppose you tell me what this is all about, Jeff MacKennon."

4

○○○○○○○○○○○

You don't believe my story?"

"No."

Jeff raised an eyebrow and appeared calmly amused. "Cynical, aren't you?"

"In this case, why shouldn't I be?" But her voice stayed unflustered and even. "It would have taken only a moment to call and tell me that you were coming in person."

"And spoil the surprise?" He laughed, obviously enjoying the moment. "What if I did it on impulse?"

"You—act on impulse? Never. You always know exactly where you're going and when you'll make your move—or don't you recall telling me that?"

He shrugged, unruffled. "Maybe I have an impulsive side which I keep well hidden, even from my closest friends." He waited for her reaction, saw the glimmer of interest in her eyes, and pressed on. "You thought you had me pegged all the way, didn't you? Come on," he coaxed with infectious humor, "admit it."

It was useless to fight it; she found herself smiling a little. "More or less."

"All right, just for that I'm going to keep you guessing. However, I meant it when I said I was here to study your program report for possible funding."

"And for no other reason, I suppose?"

"Not for the reasons you might think," he said, letting sarcasm put an edge on his words.

"So now you think you can read my mind."

"Okay, let's see if I'm right. You figured I was out here to do a little political sowing, and maybe have some fun on the side, and perhaps even with you. How's that?"

"Not bad."

"Did you stop to think of yet another possibility?"

"Which is . . . ?"

"That there was a good feeling between us the last time I saw you and that, just maybe, I wanted us to recapture that same feeling and hopefully take it from there."

It was his gentleness that stuck in her mind. "I haven't forgotten, but . . ."

"Yes, I know—please don't recite your declaration of independence to me again, Monica. I think I know it by heart. Let me suggest an alternative. Why waste a lot of time wondering *what if?* Why don't we start all over again on a friendly basis and see what happens?

Meanwhile, I'll be concentrating on your report and we'll wait and see what really does happen between us. Who knows, maybe we'll find that, after the dust settles, we really don't like each other. But I wouldn't bet on it."

"What if we're faced with the same old problem?" she asked, fighting the pleasure she got just looking at him. "What then?"

"As you said, we'll survive—we're both very strong people." He slowly lifted his hands, palms up, urging her to take and hold them. Once again, it wasn't a threatening or demanding gesture; it was merely a gentle, friendly supplication. "Come on, let's make a start."

She reached out and clasped his hands, praying that the grip would stay loose and the mood would remain light. "All right, let's try," she said, happy with the way her poise didn't desert her. "Thanks for taking a personal interest in the funding. How's that for openers?"

"Pretty good. Tell me, how appreciative are you?"

"That you want to help with my program?" She couldn't help emphasizing the last word. "Very."

"Then I know a way you can show it."

"Oh?" She was afraid for a moment, but the grip on her hands remained as it had been. "How?"

"Have lunch with me."

"What happened, did they forget to feed you on the plane?"

"They piled a bunch of stuff in front of me, but I wasn't hungry. Please, let me take you to lunch, and I promise to talk about nothing but business—as grim as that might be for the digestion." He smiled his slow, provocative smile. "I'm really very hungry now."

"All right, let's have lunch—but it'll have to be a working lunch."

"It doesn't have to be *all* business, you know."

"I'm afraid it does. I've already made a date to eat lunch with some of the kids in my program, Jeff. Sorry."

"All right,'" he said, sighing, "what do we eat?"

She slowly slipped her hands from his and bent to retrieve the brown paper sack. "Of course, if I had known we'd be sharing lunch today, I would have packed some beluga and champagne, but"—she held aloft the plain little bag—"since I wasn't prepared to entertain you in style, all I can offer you is half my sandwich. Eat it or starve," she laughed.

"You drive a hard bargain," he murmured. "Okay, since I don't have much of a choice, it's a deal."

The day was warm; cloudless, sunny, beautiful. As they strolled across the grassy promenade leading to the state legislative offices, she glanced at his profile. Lord, there should be a law against anybody looking so damned sensual in broad daylight. She was shaken, and she knew it; surprise wasn't the only response he'd wrung out of her when he walked into her office. She had a hard fight on her hands, she realized—and not so much with him as with herself. She asked abruptly, "Will you be staying only a day or two, as you mentioned to Holly?"

He turned to look at her. "That depends." So that

there would be no mistake in his meaning, he explained, "Until I take a look at your report I really won't know for sure."

"I think you'll find that it's complete and concise," she said without hesitation.

"I didn't mean to imply that it wasn't, Monica. I have to study it carefully, however, before I put my opinion on the line before the allocations committee. Don't be so defensive."

"Was I?" Her gaze was level and without guile. "You're reading me all wrong, Jeff. I have no reason to be defensive about my program. I've already been told by experts that the project is solid and creative."

"Tell me, are *you* satisfied with what you've done?"

"No, because I feel there's so much more to be done in this field of education."

"Okay," he said, smiling at her spirited comeback, "let me take a good, hard, dispassionate look at your report and I promise to issue an honest recommendation. What do you say?"

"I say, follow me," she answered, squaring her shoulders.

They climbed the wide stairs leading to one wing of the historic capitol building and went inside to walk along the labyrinth of marbled corridors. When Monica stopped in front of the door of an assemblyman's office, Jeff glanced for a moment at the name inscribed on the highly polished brass doorplate. "Do you know Assemblyman Rogers?" she asked, noting the recognition in his eyes.

"I've had some contact with him, yes," Jeff said, but gave no other information.

Assemblyman Rogers was in his office, busy as the devil at his desk, when Jeff and Monica walked in. The office was not much larger than Monica's, and an improvised desk had been set aside in an alcove beyond for a young woman. The girl, obviously of high-school age, turned and smiled when she saw Monica. "Hi!"

"Hello, Judy," Monica replied, and then she turned her attention to Assemblyman Alexander Rogers, a young, bookish-looking man with the proverbial harried air of the dedicated public servant. His smile, however, was as broad as it was genuine. "Monica, glad to see you!" He walked around his desk and peered at her companion. "Jeff MacKennon, isn't it? What brings you down from the heights of Olympian Washington to this part of the empire?"

"It's all part of the same empire, don't forget," Jeff said, grasping the offered hand warmly. "How have you been, Al?"

"Overworked as usual, but what else is new?" he laughed. "Tell me, any specific reason you're here in Sacramento?"

"Department of Education business, that's all," Jeff replied with just the right touch of friendly civility— and nothing more.

But Al Rogers was too intrigued to let it go at that. "You wouldn't, by sheer chance, be here to to spread around some of your department's millions for worthy local educational purposes, would you?"

All of Jeff's political training was evident in his careful but charming smile. "I might be."

"Well, if you are," the assemblyman suggested,

nodding toward Monica and then to Judy in the little alcove, "I can't think of a better place to start than Monica's work-pay program for deserving high-school students. It's a wonderful program. As you can see, Monica's even had the kids jump right into the program as volunteers, with the promise of money to come. But now . . ." He stopped for a moment and then shook his head as if remembering something. "But then, you must know all about Monica's project suffering a cutback, because I wrote you a long memo about it, didn't I?"

"Yes, I read it with great interest," Jeff replied quietly, not looking Monica's way. "That's partly why I'm here."

"Good!" Al Rogers turned to Monica. "If Jeff promises to help, then believe me, Monica, you'll see some action."

Aside from nodding and smiling, Monica remained noncommittal. She hadn't known that Jeff had received any direct communication concerning the cutback, and when they left Assemblyman Rogers' office her surprise grew. With Judy in tow, they visited other state senate and assembly offices, and it became plain that Jeff had been in contact with a number of legislators; what's more, it was obvious that he was on a first-name basis with more than a few of them. As they made the rounds of offices, with a growing flock of Monica's youngsters trailing along, she was an eyewitness to the vast extent of Jeff's political polish and astuteness. He had done his homework well before coming to Sacramento; he never stumbled over a name or a statistic, especially if the matter concerned education. And Monica noticed something else, too. The legislators they visited were all seasoned politicians themselves, but without exception they greeted Jeff MacKennon with subtle deference and respect. Monica began to wonder: Was it the man himself that they liked and admired, or was it Jeff's reputation that impressed nearly everybody? Even in California, it seemed as if everyone knew that Jeff MacKennon was destined for nothing but the highest levels of the White House itself.

As they settled down on the patio where they were to eat their lunches, the crowd of young people formed a circle around Monica and Jeff. "Everybody seems to have something to eat except me," Jeff quipped, sitting astride a wooden bench. "Am I going to be left to starve?"

Monica could hear a guffaw or two coming from the crowd around her. "I promised to share my lunch with you, remember?"

"Yeah, that's right." Gone was the polished but careful public image; the smile was warm and intimate now. "Beluga and champagne, wasn't it?"

The laughs were louder this time. "Peanut butter and alfalfa sprouts, you mean," Monica chided, handing over half her sandwich.

He held it in his hand, inspecting it. "On stone-ground bread, of course."

"That's right. Eat it—it's good for you. You're in the health-food belt now, remember?" But she was smiling as she took a bite of the sandwich. She saw that he was still hesitating, looking dubiously at his half. "Jeff, I know you're used to long, leisurely lunches at exclusive men's clubs, but the students want to ask you some questions and they have a short lunch break. So why don't you dig into that sandwich?"

"Fine—but I think I'll have a problem."

"What problem?"

"How can I talk with peanut butter stuck to the roof of my mouth?"

"You're the politician—improvise! Remember, it's peanut butter or starvation."

One of the youngsters saved the moment by offering Jeff a container of orange juice to wash down the peanut butter. Jeff graciously accepted the gift; when the sandwich and juice were gone, he turned his attention to the crowd of students. "First, I'd like to hear from *you*," he stated, gazing out at the group. "I want to know why you're taking part in this particular project."

Several voices spoke at once and Monica watched Jeff take control of the session. He listened carefully, gave each student time to be heard and then encouraged them with more questions or advice. They knew of his status in Washington because all of them were avidly interested in current events and national politics; Jeff, in turn, addressed the youngsters as knowledgeable individuals, refusing to talk down to them or lecture them in a condescending manner. He seemed impressed with their enthusiasm and their common sense; they opened up to him, instinctively trusting him, even eventually discussing their financial problems. For instance, how could they continue to take part in the program, even though they received valuable school credits, when some of them might be forced to make a choice between important experiences in government and the need to earn money in part-time jobs to help cover the mounting costs of their education?

Monica saw yet another facet of Jeff's character. He seemed genuinely moved by the students' gritty determination to continue in government service, no matter what the sacrifice. Was he really interested, or was he just putting on a public display? She listened as he spoke insistently. "I know it's difficult when you don't have enough money, but *don't give up.* There are ways—you just have to find them—the opportunities won't come looking for *you.* Work *with* the system, not against it, because it's there to help you, believe me."

Was this the Washington playboy and political climber talking? Monica wondered. It couldn't be; his sincerity reached out and turned everybody into a believer. Damn him, why did he always have to be so unpredictable, so full of surprises? With a slight shock, she realized that he had brought the session to a close. Some of the youngsters lingered for a few more words with Jeff, but soon Monica was left alone with him on the sunny patio. "That was quite an exhibition," she said with genuine admiration. "I'm thoroughly surprised."

"Because I know something about education?"

"Because you know so much."

"Why shouldn't I be well-informed? After all, I *am* the director of funding for a rather large number of educational programs," he murmured, managing to make the remark sound flippant.

CAPITOL AFFAIR

"I'm serious, Jeff. You were sincerely concerned with the youngsters' problems, so don't try to joke it away."

He still held the juice container in his hand. Balancing it for a second, he took aim and then dropped the empty container smack into the center of a concrete trash receptacle at the far end of the patio. "Not having enough money for a decent education—or for food or clothes or a date—is no joke for somebody growing up. Don't read me wrong."

"Yet somehow you managed to get a marvelous education without money."

"I would have preferred to have Daddy or Mommy write out a nice fat check to pay for my studies, but I had worse problems than merely being poor," he said lightly, straddling the bench again and keeping an amused smile on his face. "I was one of the pathetic orphans-of-the-storm."

"Adopted?"

"No, abandoned, actually, and then brought up in foster homes." He laughed at her expression. "Hey, don't look so sorrowful, Monica. The only reason I brought up the subject was that I wanted you to know I understand how important your work-pay program can be to a kid."

"You mean it would have made it easier for you if such a program had existed when you were going to school."

"Right. But instead, I found other ways, as I told the group."

Other ways? Scholarships or wealthy benefactors— or benefactresses? A little ashamed of her thoughts,

Monica reminded herself that it was none of her business how he'd acquired his education and polish. She brushed some crumbs from her hand and said, "I should be getting back to work. I told you that the report is ready. Do you want to see it now?"

"I'll walk you back to your office and pick it up."

"Do you want to go over it with me this afternoon?"

"No, I don't think so. First, let me read through it, and then we can discuss it tomorrow, okay?"

"That sounds fine."

"Of course, I won't be able to read the report in *too* much detail tonight."

"Why not?"

"Because I have something important to do."

"More important than the report?" she inquired pointedly.

"*I* think so," he murmured, taking her arm and leading her from the patio to the green promenade stretching across to her office building. The day was so beautiful that she resented not being stupendously happy; however, Jeff's allusion to the struggles of his younger days had disturbed her. "Jeff, do you resent the fact that you and I started life so differently?"

"What on earth are you talking about?"

She didn't know herself, not really. "I was just thinking aloud, I suppose. I was wondering if that's why you're sometimes so . . . so . . . well, almost unkind to me." She knew immediately that she had chosen her words badly, and tried to explain. "Sometimes I get the feeling that you're almost angry with me—and I don't know why. I have to tell you that I have one hell of a time keeping up with your moods.

One moment you snap at me and say that I'm stubborn and childish . . ."

"Monica . . ."

"And the next moment you're manhandling me . . ."

"Monica, please . . ."

"And then you put on a sincere exhibition like the one you pulled a few minutes ago." She inclined her head to see him better in the brilliant sunshine. "You know something, Jeff MacKennon, I think you're a little crazy," she summarized, laughing.

"That, coming from a bona fide maverick like you?"

"Touché, my friend."

They walked a few more paces before he answered. "You know, I might have resented a person like you for what you are—rich, good family background, deep roots and all the rest—when I was much younger. But I've taught myself not to envy. Envy, resentment, self-pity—those things just drain a person's energy."

"At least," she said, smiling, "you've never accused me of being envious, resentful or self-pitying, thank God!"

"Right," he agreed, "but I still have a problem I can't solve, and it *does* concern you. My problem is that I like you too much exactly the way you are."

"I wish you hadn't said that."

"I think it's a nice thing to say to somebody," he murmured, with a hint of wistfulness. "Anyway, it needs saying."

She decided the subject should be dropped.

"There's something I'd like to know, and I might as well be blunt about it, Jeff."

"Ask me."

"You know quite a bit more about my program than you want to admit, don't you? I didn't miss those remarks from Al Rogers and the others that you've been in contact with them. Why didn't you tell me?"

"It was nothing special, just part of my job."

"I don't believe you."

"Listen, I have contacts all over the country, and I make it my business to know people in government, to familiarize myself with their pet projects and to keep all that information filed away in the back of my mind."

A facile answer, she thought, but it was too pat. "You wouldn't care to explain that in a little more detail, would you?"

"I will, but not now. Maybe tonight might be a better time."

"But I thought you had something important— something more important than reading my report— to do tonight."

"I do," he replied. "I'm taking you to supper."

"Jeff, I can't."

"Yes, you can. Anyway," he said with a smile, "I think you owe me something for forcing me to eat that peanut-butter sandwich."

"Was it really so bad?"

"It was lousy," he laughed, "but don't think I'm complaining! However, tonight I want something solid *and* unhealthy, and you're going to join me."

"We both promised to keep things friendly and easy. . . ."

"And we're going to have a friendly-and-easy eve-ning together."

But she still protested. "Can't we stick to business?"

"No, we can't," he stated flatly, "and we both know it. Eight o'clock at your apartment?"

Up until that moment, she had been rather proud of the way she had kept up the charade. She had acted and reacted in a fairly reasonable and dignified man-ner, and nobody watching them could have guessed that she—a successful career woman who had sur-vived the terrible trauma of sudden widowhood and who had blithely celebrated her thirtieth birthday last year without a qualm—was on the brink of letting herself slide into a surefire emotional trap. Still fighting and struggling, she waited for one moment . . . and then another . . . and then slowly nodded and said, "Eight o'clock will be fine."

After Jeff stopped by the office to pick up the report and then left, Monica sat at her desk and stared into space. "Have you fallen asleep with your eyes open, or have you become catatonic?"

Monica flinched and looked up at Holly. "I was thinking, that's all."

"Some thoughts! Monica, you looked spooked again."

Monica felt too drained to deny anything. Instead, she nodded toward the cluster of packages Holly had just plopped on her desk. "Are you expecting Christ-mas to arrive early this year?"

"Oh, these are just a few things I needed, that's all."

"How was the pizza?"

"As a matter of fact, I skipped lunch altogether. Who needs the extra calories, right?"

"Holly, you hate shopping."

"So I thought I might as well get it over with on my lunch hour, see?"

"Holly!"

"Okay," she groaned, surrendering with a grimace, "so I found something to keep me busy and out of the office for a while. Go ahead and sue me!"

"But, two hours? Holly, you didn't have to do that, you know."

"I don't understand why you're complaining, Monica! Lord, if I had the chance to be alone with that man—if I weren't already in love with Gavin, of course—I sure as hell wouldn't be protesting. And by the way, your Mr. MacKennon isn't just plain sexy, you know. That's the understatement of the year! Why didn't you tell me that he's a delicious twelve-course meal for the eyes?"

"I suppose there's a lot about him that I didn't tell you."

Taking a better look at Monica, Holly suddenly realized something was very wrong. "Look, I've been kidding around, but I think something serious has happened and I'm sorry, okay?" When Monica kept silent, Holly persisted, "What happened, did you two have a clash or something? Tell me the truth now, Monica. You and Jeff MacKennon aren't just casual business acquaintances, are you? I mean, back in Washington . . ."

"We didn't have a fight today," Monica mumbled, confused and unhappy. "For a change, we got along very well. We spent most of the time talking to the kids in the program, and Jeff was brilliant and outgoing and the students loved him. I had an enlightening, worthwhile afternoon with Jeff MacKennon."

"Monica, for heaven's sake—I don't understand!"

"I'm upset because he asked me to have supper with him."

"So—that's *bad?*"

"Holly . . ."

Monica placed her fingertips over her eyes and bowed her head in pure weariness and distress. Really worried now, Holly quickly reached her friend and put an arm around Monica's shoulders. "What's the matter, Monica? Please, can't you tell me and let me help?"

"I'm letting it start all over again," was all that Monica could manage to say. "And deep down inside, that's exactly what I want," she added, all in a rush and making little sense. "That's why I'm so miserable, Holly."

"Was it entirely your own idea to call me and ask for financial help, or did you need a little coaxing from a person or persons unknown?"

The tinkle of fine china and crystal accompanied Jeff's droll question. Their table, secreted in a Victorian cupola with a stained-glass roof, permitted the most discreet conversation. He gazed at Monica across the beautifully appointed table and persisted, "Well, tell me?"

"Does it really make any difference?"

"Yes, or I wouldn't have asked."

Be honest with him, she told herself. "I was desperate to find a way to get the program formally started this summer, and I was talking it over with Holly and Gavin . . ."

"They're a team, I gather."

"Oh, yes, very much in love, and perfect together."

He leaned back; his eyes sparkled like jet-fire diamonds. "Go on."

"And I suddenly thought of you. But . . . I might as well confess that I didn't want to call you. I gave in and phoned you, finally, when Holly and Gavin reminded me that the program was too important to lose."

Now she had his complete attention. "That's very interesting."

Monica put her fork on her plate; the gourmet food had passed through her lips without taste. "I don't see anything particularly interesting about it. After all, I finally called you, didn't I?"

"Sure, but what I find interesting is that you probably wouldn't have approached me if Holly and Gavin hadn't leaned on you. Why?"

"You know how I feel about exchanging professional 'favors,' Jeff."

"In government, that's a foolish, even naive way to feel."

"In government, the way I was taught, anyway, that's the ideal way to function."

"Oh, yes, *ideals.*" With a wave of his hand he easily brushed that possibility away. "Government is a hard-nosed *business,* just like any other business."

"Excuse me," she interjected, "but I thought we were discussing government, not politics."

CAPITOL AFFAIR

The directness of her little jab pleased him. "Spoken like a true daughter of 'Somber' Judge Lewis!"

"Thanks," she countered, smiling back at him with ease. "I consider that a great compliment."

He raised his glass and waited. She also picked up her glass. They saluted each other in silence. "Monica Lewis," he finally murmured, as if he were testing the sound of her name. "May I ask you something personal?"

"As long as it's not too personal and outrageous, why not?"

"When did you decide to keep your own name— before or after your marriage to Jim Bloomquist?"

She was rather surprised by the simplicity of the question. "I don't remember, really, probably because I was married such a short time before Jim was killed in South America." She saw something in his eyes that she mistook for astonishment. "Didn't you know his plane crashed while he was on a fact-finding tour down there?"

"Yes, I knew."

She hesitated, not because of any lachrymose memories of her late husband, but because she didn't want any shadows to descend on Jeff and herself. The evening had been smooth and easy so far, and she yearned to hold on to the good feeling between them. "Jeff, I'm beginning to suspect that you know a lot about my life, past and present. For instance, you knew my home address. You didn't have to be told where I lived."

"A small detail which you shouldn't begrudge a friend."

"All right, then, let's see if familiarity works both ways. May I ask you a question?"

"Of course," he said, smiling, "and please make it as personal and outrageous as you want."

"How long do you think it will be before you achieve what you want the most?"

His eyes narrowed, and it was difficult to tell whether it was from a positive emotion or temper. "Which particular desire are you talking about, Monica?"

"Why, the one most important to you, of course," she replied, feigning wide-eyed surprise. "I'm talking about the post on the White House staff."

Incredibly, he seemed disinterested. "That offer finally came through."

She was openly surprised. "It did?"

"Yes, a number of months ago."

"Well, go on. What happened?"

"I turned it down."

Now she was thoroughly shocked. "Why, for heaven's sake?"

"Many reasons, really."

"I don't believe this!" She remembered the rumors rampant in Washington circles concerning his burning desire to climb to the very top of the political ladder. "Everybody assumed—"

"Then everybody was wrong," he said, dismissing the subject brusquely. "Don't believe every rumor you hear about me, Monica—professional or personal. Find out the facts for yourself."

He had flung her a challenge, but she didn't choose to follow through on it. Instead, she suggested lightly,

"Oh, well, I guess I made a very human mistake. I thought, 'where there's smoke,' et cetera, et cetera."

"Not necessarily," he asserted, pushing his coffee cup away with an impatient and intensely male gesture. "Sometimes it's best just to let the fire smolder until it burns out." He relaxed as suddenly as he had tensed. "I'm sure that coffee in your cup is as cold as ice. Should I tell the waiter to bring some fresh coffee?"

She stopped playing with the finely curved handle of her own cup. "No, I don't think I want any more."

"Let's leave, then. . . ."

The night had turned cold and the sky was full of pinpoint stars. As they waited for the parking attendant to bring the car around, Jeff reached out to hold her, warming her. She leaned against him quite naturally, letting him shield her from the chill that hung in the air. Soon she was seated beside him in the soothing comfort of his rented sports car, his body pressed closely alongside hers. When he headed the car in the direction of her apartment, she let her head fall on his shoulder without a word. She knew she would ask him up to her apartment, and she knew that she wanted to make love with him. Beyond that, she didn't know what would happen and, for once, she didn't care. She wasn't ready yet to admit that what she felt for Jeff was dangerously close to love; she needed time later to sort out her conflicting feelings for him. And it wasn't just a case of throwing caution to the winds, because somehow or other the funding problem would be solved, and the ultimate solution was out of both Jeff's hands and her own. Right now she could acknowledge only her intense desire for the man on whose shoulder her head was resting. She didn't like mysteries, and he was an enigma, perhaps the only truly impenetrable person she had ever encountered in her life. She wanted to dig beneath his cool exterior tonight, deep down to the raw core of him. She needed him tonight, and she was going to have him, come hell, guilt or misery tomorrow.

He stopped the car in front of her apartment and turned to face her. She searched for his mouth, and found it quickly. Twisting her body, she made contact with him from his chest to his groin. He reacted in swift spasms, grazing her back and shoulders in stimulating circles with a friction that threatened to burn straight through the thin stuff of her clothes. She clung to him, and then felt herself pushed away. Lost in feeling, she vaguely expected to hear him moan that he was too impatient to stay in the car, that they should go to her apartment, that he was ready to explode. . . .

Instead, he opened the window a crack, drew some air into his lungs, and closed his eyes for a second. Then he looked across at Monica. She knew he was looking at her in the darkness because the many tiny lights from the dashboard were reflected across the jet of his eyes. "What's wrong?" she finally whispered, still in a daze, but beginning to sense that he had thrust her away with sudden finality, not passion. She leaned to place her fingers around the back of his neck, just where the black hair curled, to urge him to come closer to her again. "Hold me a little while longer, please." He didn't move. "Don't you think I want you enough? But, I do . . . so very, very much."

"No doubts?"

"None . . . not tonight."

He seemed to recede deeper into the shadows. "That's not good enough for me."

She was too puzzled to speak for a moment. What was this, some kind of cruel game? "You're punishing me a little for the past, aren't you?"

"No."

"Are you waiting for me to beg, to soothe your ego?"

"God, *no.*" The laugh was no more than a grunt, short and cutting. "So you think I'm capable of *that,* too?" He shifted, trying to make out her face in the almost total darkness. "While you're at it, why don't you also accuse me of imagining something really nasty, like an exchange of your 'favors' for a good word to my funding committee?"

"I would never think such a disgusting thing," she hissed, too stunned to shout or cry out. "I know the final decision is up to the committee, not you."

"Well, I suppose I should be grateful for that one vote of confidence, anyway. At least you don't think I'm a hopeless sexist and lecher."

Her shock was starting to wear off and an embarrassed fury was taking its place. "What are you talking about? Tell me—please."

"Okay, I'll risk it." Still, his hand shot out to grab her fingers in his fist to keep her from bolting out of the car, just in case. "I'm not sure yet just what you feel for me, how much you trust me—and maybe you're not really sure, either. Maybe you're confused, and I don't want to add to your confusion or do anything that might make you feel even more uneasy about me later." Monica listened mutely, unable to speak. "And for me, I know that tomorrow, after we've spent the night together, I don't want to face an iceberg; I don't want to find out that you've conveniently forgotten everything we might say to each other tonight. I can't just walk into a room tomorrow and see you looking right through me." His tone, which had been almost pleading, suddenly changed as he tightened his grasp on her fingers and snapped, "Now, if all you want is a nice friendly evening with a guy, casual and laid-back —then, come on!" He flung open his door, put more pressure on his grip, and pulled her toward him until she fell halfway across the seat. "But I'm warning you, Monica, if we happen to confess a lot of feelings to each other sometime during the night, good and honest and special feelings, I won't put up with any guilt from you in the morning."

"Let go of me," she finally cried, cutting off the flow of brutal words. "I don't want to hear any more." Frantic now, she tried to free herself from his numbing, paralyzing grip. But it was useless; he held on even tighter. "Monica, if it came to a final choice between loving me and your career, what would you do? How long would you keep up the lie?" Suddenly he didn't want to overpower her anymore. His fist opened and he let her hand slip away. There was a quiet, pleading quality to his words again. "Would you be able to admit you made a mistake and return with me to Washington, where you belong?"

She didn't even realize that he wasn't holding on to her. "So that's how you see it! Either way, I'm just a hypocrite, aren't I?"

"I didn't say that—I'm only spelling out some of the doubts which are going to stare you in the face tomorrow and the day after and the day after that, dammit."

"I don't need you to think for me or feel for me or plan my life for me," she declared. "I didn't chase after you in Washington and I didn't ask you to come to California! I asked for your professional help, not a personal attack, and—"

"And yet, a few minutes ago, you said you wanted me—without any doubts, I think you said. Should I understand that you didn't mean that personally, either?"

She was speechless; however, not for too long. "You're hateful, do you know that?"

He spoke very quietly, twisting the knife. "Why, because I reminded you that you wanted to sleep with me?"

Then she moved fast. She was out of the car and up the stairs to her apartment before he could move to stop her. She stepped inside swiftly, slammed the front door shut, and locked it. Then she leaned against the door, guarding it, until she heard his car race away. Willing herself to stop trembling, she went directly to the side table which served as a compact bar, and without even glancing at the decanter label, poured a good splash of liquor into an old-fashioned glass. Carrying it with both hands, she let her purse slip out from under her arm and collapsed on the sofa before taking a sip from the glass. Scotch, of all things. She hated Scotch, but she willed herself to take another swallow of the stuff.

It was late and she knew that she would have to be at her desk early in the morning, but she sat for a long time, rolling the glass gently between her palms. Finally she went into the kitchen and poured the remainder of the drink down the drain. She walked into the bedroom, stripped off her clothes and left them piled on the floor, and then got into bed, although she knew it would be useless to close her eyes.

It had been an evening of half-truths, half-lies, and, worst of all, deep, deep hurt. She felt frustrated and ashamed, and she felt angry and defiant, too. And sometime near dawn, she began to cry, but in spite of the tears, she didn't feel any better when the early sunlight crept through the windows.

In the morning, Monica took extra care with her clothes, hair and makeup, hoping to wipe away the strain left by last night's havoc. Arriving at work, she hesitated when she reached the small entryway to her office. Why was she afraid? There was no need for fear, none at all. Sometime after sunrise, when the full glare of daylight had chased away all the ghosts, came hard cold reason: today would be a business day just like any other. It didn't make any difference that Jeff MacKennon would be in her office all day. She would control her emotions, her actions, and if necessary, she would control him, too. She pushed open the door and came face to face with Jeff MacKennon.

He was comfortably seated alongside her desk, concentrating on the program report. "Good morning," he said nonchalantly.

Monica looked around for Holly, but Jeff was alone in the office. "Good morning," she answered curtly. "Has Holly been in yet?"

"No, not since I arrived."

"What time did you get here?"

"An hour ago." A trace of a frown appeared. "I believe in starting work as early as possible."

She was going to say something in return, but Holly came bouncing through the door. "Oh, hello, Mr. MacKennon!" She gave him her brightest smile. "Hi, Monica, sorry I'm a little late."

"No problem," Monica assured her friend. "I just got here myself." She sat down at her desk. "When you're ready, Holly, we can begin reviewing the report with Mr. MacKennon."

"Oh, sure."

"That is," Monica continued, with a nod at Jeff, "if you've had the time to glance through it."

"I've gone through it in depth, as a matter of fact." He closed the folder and held it lightly in his hand. "I found that I couldn't sleep last night, so instead I sat up most of the night and read it."

She didn't look at him this time. To Holly she said, "I haven't put up the coffee yet. Sorry."

"Oh, that's all right," Holly said, beginning to feel the frigid vibrations between Monica and Jeff. Last night's "supper" must have been a disaster! "I'll take care of it."

Monica shifted some papers around on her desk

and cleared it so that she could spread her copy of the report on the surface. She kept her eyes fastened to the text. Jeff remained silent, opening the report again and turning the pages at a slow pace. Holly returned with the coffee mugs to find them silently ignoring each other. "Black okay, Mr. Mac-Kennon?"

"Call me Jeff and, yes, black is fine."

Holly handed Monica her cup with an inquiring look that Jeff wasn't supposed to notice. "Here's yours, Monica."

"Thanks. Now, shall we get to work?"

"Of course," Jeff agreed, and then drank some of his coffee. "That's why I'm here, remember?"

All right, Monica warned herself, *let it pass.* The three of them worked in polite, cold silence, speaking only when necessary. That is, Monica and Jeff maintained a strained, monosyllabic discourse; Holly tried to inject some humor and ease into the session. No dice, since the other two seemed intent on discussing only facts and figures. Around noon, Holly finally began to wilt under all the tension. "I really think we should break for lunch, huh?"

Monica momentarily came out of her trance. "Good idea. Why don't we call and have a pizza delivered?"

Holly, shocked, stole a glance at Jeff. "Well, I really don't think that Mr. MacKennon—sorry, I mean, Jeff—would want *pizza* for lunch, Monica!" She couldn't stifle a nervous giggle. "I'm sure he's used to a more elegant—"

"But you've been craving pizza—you told me so,"

Monica stubbornly interrupted, "so why all the fuss? Anyway, pizza is very healthy and nutritious."

Holly gaped at her friend's perverse remark, but it was Jeff who made the decision. "Pizza is fine with me, Holly. Beats peanut-butter sandwiches, anytime."

Since Monica seemed to have lost her capacity to speak for a moment, Holly suggested, "It might be better if I run down and get the pizza myself. If we have decided to have pizza for lunch, I mean."

Monica came to life again. "Just call and have the pizza delivered, please, Holly."

Lord, they must have had a *doozy* of a fight! Holly was sure of it now. But she was desperate to leave the electrically charged atmosphere. "Oh, I don't mind going. It's such a beautiful day and I really want to stretch my legs," she said over her shoulder, already making a dash for the door. "Anyway, the pizza place is right on the corner and I'll be back in five minutes flat."

When the door closed, Monica remained rigidly at her desk, gazing across the room at nothing. Jeff returned to the report for a moment, but finally broke into her thoughts. "The way you're acting doesn't make sense to me."

"But it does to me," she replied, straightening some papers. "All I want to do is get this business over with so you can return to Washington. Then, if I get the money, I can continue with my program and I will truly appreciate everything you've done for me. I will also tell everyone, loudly and clearly so that it will reach all the way to Washington, how wonderful and totally cooperative you were, so that your political image will go up another notch. We'll both have gotten what we wanted," she emphasized, pulling out a sheet covered with figures and applying herself to reading it with deliberate curtness. "Now, if you'll just look at this projection, you'll see that each student will receive—"

"And what if the allocations committee, by some slim chance, doesn't grant you the money?" he asked, ignoring the sheet that she was holding out for him to read. "What then?"

She carefully laid the paper back on her desk because she saw that her hand was shaking a bit. "Then I'll go on planning next year's programs here in Sacramento, where I intend to live and be happy and work for a long, *long* time."

The report fell out of his hands and onto the desk with a sharp crack. "I have a real urge to shake some common sense into you!"

"I'm quite satisfied with my own common sense, and your urges don't interest me. Shall we get back to work?"

"No, I don't think so," he said after a long pause. "I have all the information I need now." He gathered the assorted papers together and slipped them into a handsome leather attaché case. He headed for the door, but stopped before leaving. "I have just a polite request, from one professional to another. I'm meeting with some members of the governor's staff for drinks. Would you like to come along?"

"Why?" She slowly stood and leaned forward, spreading her palms on the desktop. "Is it necessary for your image to show up with a woman clinging to your arm, even at a simple date for drinks?" She had controlled herself superbly up to this moment, but she felt her resolve beginning to slip away. The hurt of last night's rejection flared through her mind, wounding her all over again. Of all the insults he had ever hurled at her, that one had been the most painful. She resorted to sarcasm as a momentary balm, but she wasn't very proud of herself for doing it. "What will you hope to prove, Jeff MacKennon, that you had an easy time making it with a local—even on a rushed business trip to a backwater like Sacramento?"

He looked like he wanted to say something brutal, something lacerating, but he managed to swallow the words. "Nothing sexist or personal intended, Monica. I mistakenly thought that, for once, you might be interested in a mutual business invitation."

"No, thanks. Ambition has never been one of my vices."

He waited a beat or two. "I'll let you know about this"—he nodded toward the attaché case in his hand—"as soon as possible."

"Yes." Then she added another, "Thank-you." And then she said definitively, "Good-bye."

When she returned, Holly found Monica leaning on the desk, but her gaze was turned away, toward the window. "Say, where's Mr. MacKennon?"

Monica didn't look around. "He left, quite suddenly." Almost as an afterthought, she added over her shoulder, "You were right, Holly, it *is* a beautiful day."

Oh, my God, Holly thought, the woman was raving and probably hiding a flood of tears! "Yes, it's lovely outside. What about the report?"

"Jeff has all the information he needs."

Holly let the hot pizza carton slip out of her arms, dropping it with a resounding thump on the desk. "Well, that's rotten! I bought an extra-large pizza with sausage and pepperoni, because I thought he—"

"You were right about something else, too," Monica said, turning around. "Jeff MacKennon *did* prefer caviar and champagne to ordinary pizza." Holly, expecting to find Monica's eyes hazed with tension and tears, was startled to see her friend's face absolutely expressionless. "Come on, Holly, I suddenly feel very hungry. Let's dig into this before it gets cold, shall we?"

5

The beautifully perfect day had turned into a strangely muggy night, almost unheard of in Sacramento at this time of year. Monica sat in front of her television—stripped down to shorts and T-shirt, and clutching a wine spritzer in her hand—staring at a sitcom, but seeing and hearing nothing. Her mind was totally involved with Jeff.

Last night's rebuff stung a little less now, and she could see some logic to his explanations. Still, where did that leave her? She faced a hard fact: she had, like a damned fool, let herself fall in love with him. Another hard fact: she was sexually attracted to him to the extent of being almost totally distracted. So what? Those two facts continued to add up to absolutely nothing, she told herself for the tenth time. Stretching, she glanced at the nonsense issuing from the television and then rose to get some more wine.

Monica stopped as she passed her large picture window, and looked out at the Capitol's gilded dome in the far distance. It was flooded with lights and it shone like a golden beacon. She leaned against the window frame, and once again she began to rethink the whole sorry situation. One thing was certain: she loved California and she never wanted to leave it. Yet she loved Jeff MacKennon, too, and his heart and mind and future were in Washington. He was ambitious to the exclusion of everything and everybody else, including herself. She couldn't delude herself on that last point; no matter what Jeff felt for her—and she suspected that he loved her in his own unique way—his career would always come first. Well, no, thanks! she mused. She had been that route before, and she didn't want any part of that misery again.

To be fair, she remembered that he had seemed very sincere when he'd praised her work here in Sacramento. She thought back to the afternoon they'd spent with the students; then she remembered that evening—and this afternoon—and . . . Oh, hell! Her mind was moving in circles once more and she knew she was about to have a terrible headache. With a soft curse, she shut off the television set. Another shower, perhaps? Useless; the relief would only be momentary. She wished that she had stopped at the hardware store on her way home from work and bought a large electric fan. Oh, well, she reasoned, rubbing her temples, in this unnatural heat wave all the fans in Sacramento probably had been sold anyway.

Her mouth felt dry and sticky; the wine hadn't quenched her thirst. She went to the kitchen and filled a tall glass with crushed ice, and added plain water. When the water was cold, she put the glass to her mouth and let the cold liquid trickle along her tongue and down her parched throat. It felt so wonderful that she stopped thinking about her problems for a second and concentrated instead on the sheer pleasure of quenching her hotness . . . all the way down . . . down, to the bottom of her stomach.

Somebody knocked at the door. Probably Holly and Gavin. Hopefully, a happy Holly and Gavin! Monica desperately needed something cheerful and distracting at the moment. The one thought that nagged worse than all the others was the probability that Jeff had already left Sacramento. If not today, then tomorrow morning, for sure. She opened the door . . . and found Jeff standing there. Lounging against the door frame, he spoke. "Could you offer a sexist a tall, cool drink?"

His usual impeccable neatness was slightly frayed around the edges. The dark hair—from firsthand knowledge, she remembered how soft and silky it was—looked wet at the ends and clung to his face and neck. He had obviously tugged at his collar because his tie was slightly loose. Still, the light wool suit outlined his body perfectly, and the white shirt gleamed. He looked wonderful. "What happened, did all the members of the governor's staff turn out to be teetotalers?"

His smile was pleading and vulnerable. "No, they bent their elbows at a rapid pace, but dinner dragged on and on, and it got hotter and hotter in the dining room, and we talked and talked until my tongue felt like sandpaper and . . ." He sighed and closed his eyes for a second. "Frankly, my dear and only friend in Sacramento, I'm bushed! A tall, cold drink, please?"

"Go away."

"I'm too weak to move."

"I should let you die of thirst."

"Cruel and unusual punishment, wouldn't you say?"

"Not for the way you've behaved, no. Look, I never want to see you again and I mean every word of it! Good-bye."

His hand held the door open as she tried to slam it in his face. "I came clear out of my way to seek refuge here, Monica."

"You had gall to even *think* I would let you in my apartment, Jeff MacKennon."

"Be honest, Monica, you don't mean it when you say you never want to see me again."

"Oh, don't I?"

The same maneuver was repeated; she tried to slam the door shut and he frustrated her. "Look, I'm here and I'm a dying man. If I suddenly dropped dead, how would you explain a body on your doorstep? Think of the scandal. You'd have television cameramen crawling all over the place and tomorrow morning you'd be confronted with black headlines in every newspaper in the country."

She suddenly realized that he'd had several drinks; that fact didn't help her temper. "Will you keep quiet! If you don't, you'll have *everybody else* in the neighborhood on my doorstep."

"Then everybody will know that you cruelly stood by while a poor overworked public servant dropped dead at your feet for lack of one lousy drink of water." Provocatively, the tip of his tongue passed along his lips as if he were in the last stages of acute dehydration. "I'll accept anything you happen to have in the house—juice, beer, water, anything."

Anxious to keep him quiet, she handed over the glass of ice water. "Oh, shut up and come on in."

"Thank you," he said humbly, looking quite proud of himself. "You will reap your reward in heaven for your charity and compassion."

"Will you please get inside!"

He sauntered in, and then drained the glass of water in one long gulp. "You really were thirsty, weren't you?" she observed, shutting the door and leaning on it for a moment.

He turned to smile at her. "Why do you always doubt everything I say?"

"From habit and experience," she countered dryly. "Well, now that you're here, can I offer you a chaser? A wine spritzer, or a beer?"

He shook his head, groaning. "Actually, I think I've had enough booze for one night. A refill on that ice water would be just fine, though."

"Sure?"

"Yeah," he sighed, slowly lowering himself to sit on the edge of a red leather beanbag chair.

She left him lying there, looking completely relaxed, and went into the kitchen to get him a refill. It suddenly occurred to her that she was practically naked. It had been so warm in the apartment when she'd arrived home from work that, even after a cool shower, she had donned only the skimpiest clothes, not even bothering with a bra. She was tall enough and slim enough, but she curved and rounded in all the right places and the minuscule top-and-bottom would barely cover a beanpole. So be it, she thought, carrying the glass back into the living room. He was still sprawled on the beanbag with his eyes half-closed. "Nice place you have here," he murmured. "I didn't have much of a chance to see it last night. Real California casual— very different from east-coast posh."

"Glad you feel right at home, even though it's not the 'east-coast posh' you're used to," she commented acidly. She set the glass down on the floor within his reach. "However, don't bother to make yourself *too* comfortable here."

"Funny, you always act like such a lady and you look so damned soft, but I think I'm the only one on earth who knows that you're really as tough as nails. Would you really fling me out into the cold, cold night?"

"It must be ninety degrees outside, so I don't think you'll perish." Still, he looked genuinely tired. Harmless, really. No, he looked . . . vulnerable—and as she realized that, she experienced a slight shock. She'd never imagined that Jeff MacKennon would leave himself defenseless under any circumstances! How often did he allow himself to relax in this way? Was this a rarity, a break in the pattern? She was moved to suggest, "Why don't you take off that expensive wool jacket before you melt and ruin it?"

His eyes narrowed with lazy humor. "If you also let me loosen my tie, you've got a deal."

She held out her hand. "Come on, take it off. Since it appears that nothing short of a large dynamite blast will remove you from that chair, you might as well."

He handed over the coat and then he began to tug at the knot in his tie, but he fumbled so much that she bent over him and removed it herself. The heat from his body and the smell of cologne from his skin clung to his clothes and she very quickly placed the jacket on the back of a dining-room chair. "I'll never understand why men let themselves be condemned to wearing these silly, tight nooses around their necks," she said, fingering the silk tie a bit before draping it over the jacket. "You should emancipate yourselves from such instruments of torture."

"And lose the only touch of individuality left to us in this gray-flannel world of ours?" he laughed, unbuttoning his collar. "By the way, in case I haven't mentioned it, I like your choice of clothes very much."

"If I had known you'd be dropping by, I'd have worn a nun's habit, complete with beads and cowl."

"It wouldn't have made any difference because I have a wonderful imagination."

"Don't let it work overtime."

"No need for that—I can always bank on my memory." But he seemed to be sagging, badly, from fatigue; he didn't seem to have the strength to expand on the subject. Instead, he put his hands inside his collar and rubbed his neck. "God, I'm tired."

His vulnerability was showing itself again, and once more she felt herself reacting to it. "Then stay as you are and relax. Don't try to be witty or pull any puns. Take it easy."

"I'll fall asleep." He blinked. "I don't want to do that, so talk to me."

She sat cross-legged on the floor, resting her back against the side of the sofa. The wooden floor, usually so smooth and cool, now felt hot and rough against her bare skin. "Do you have enough strength left to answer a question?"

He barely nodded. "Shoot."

"Sacramento is a very civilized city with an ample supply of public watering holes stretching all the way from posh bars to modern hotels to the airport." She leaned her head back and gazed at him through her thick lashes. "Why did you go out of your way to zero in on my apartment for a glass of water? After last night and today, I would think you'd get the picture. I don't want to see you."

"Homing instinct? A yearning to see one friendly face in a strange town?"

"Cut it out, Jeff. Why did you come here?"

"To apologize." He leaned forward, stretching out his long legs in the same fluid movement. "To ask you to forgive me—for a lot of things."

"You're joking."

"I'm dead serious."

"What is this, a new battle tactic?" They were

talking back and forth in low voices, each of them too drained and hot to argue with vehemence. "Is this the charismatic Jeff MacKennon turning on his humble I'm-just-a-misunderstood-little-lost-boy act, guaranteed to turn half the nation's female population into a quivering, shivering mass of jelly?"

"I don't often apologize for anything I say or do, so I wouldn't know what kind of act you're talking about. What I meant was that I never meant to hurt you. Yet I *have* hurt you and . . ." He stopped, groping for the right words. "I'm sorry, because that's not what I intended to do to you. Please believe me."

"Oh, Lord, I would hate to imagine what you would be capable of if you really intended to hurt me!" She almost laughed. "Look, you've tried to frustrate my efforts to advance my career, you've called me a long list of very nasty names, you're constantly blowing hot and cold, and you pulled the topper of all time last night!"

"Not with malice, Monica." He stared at her. "I pushed you away because I didn't want to see you hurt."

"How noble!"

"Why don't you give *me* a chance to talk, for a change?"

Her legs were getting cramped and her clothes, scant as they might be, were beginning to stick to her body. She eased herself down to stretch out full-length along the floor, letting her chin rest on the wood. At any other time she would have flared at him and fought back, but she didn't feel like it tonight. It must be the heat, she reasoned. Or maybe it was because she knew he hadn't been *all* wrong last night. Whichever, she wanted to remain inert, both mentally and physically, safe across the room from him, pressed against the floor from her thighs to her breasts. "Go ahead, talk."

"But will you be *listening* to me?"

"I'll listen."

He leaned back in his former position; his hand lifted his glass off the floor, but he didn't drink. "First, let's clear the air of all that junk you threw in my face a few minutes ago concerning my many female victims."

"Come on, Jeff, surely your love affairs can't all be myths."

"Not all, no," he admitted reasonably enough, "because I happen to have a healthy appreciation for sex and romance."

"The key word is 'healthy,' don't you agree?"

"Sure, but I don't fall for somebody easily or casually," he said. Then, as if to hide the secret he had just confessed, he smiled. "Be fair—you know that the majority of stories going around about me are pure nonsense. Washington gossipmongers love to exaggerate about sex. If I were half as active as they claim, when the heck would I ever get any work done?"

"Hm-m-m," she agreed drolly, "that sounds logical to me. However, *half* a zillion is still a lot."

"Okay, I'm trying to be serious and you insist on being facetious." But he continued to smile. "I've always been very selective about everything I do. Maybe that's my problem—I'm *too* selective." A frown replaced the smile. "Let's go on to another subject, something much more important."

"All right." She brushed away a hint of jealousy. Selective, was he? So what, when he could select from such a huge mob! "Carry on, since you have the floor."

"There are things I've said to you which I've regretted afterward, believe me. Last night, for instance . . . you have no idea how much I regretted it!"

"Forget about last night."

"Why should I? You thought I was punishing you because of the times I wanted you and you cut me off. . . ."

"Okay, so I blurted something stupid because I was very upset. So now we're even and it's all over."

"No, it's not. I was sincere about not wanting you to feel *anything* that might turn you against me. Hell, did that plan backfire! You're still smoldering about it—don't lie!—and I'm the one who's left with all the guilt feelings."

She was up on her knees now. "Why are we going on with this?"

"Because I have to know something." He stared her down with sheer force. "What is there about me that attracts you and repels you, both at the same time?"

"What I feel or think is none of your business."

"When you let me know what you feel and think, then it becomes my business. For instance, you think I'm pushy and ambitious, and I almost got frostbite from the look in your eyes when I told you that I was having drinks with some people from the governor's staff."

"Wouldn't you call that pushy and ambitious?"

"No, I'm just making contacts. It's a very necessary part of my job. And, if necessary, there's nothing immoral or treacherous in asking others for help. Tell me," he said, tensing in his anxiety to get the point across to her, "didn't it help *you* to know *me* when you were so desperately searching for emergency funding for your program? Did you feel you were compromising yourself in some dirty way?"

"Professionally, no," she shot back at him.

"Then what's the problem?"

"Get this straight, once and for all, Jeff MacKennon. The problem started when you turned a professional transaction into a personal indulgence. The problem started," she repeated and emphasized, "when you came to California."

"That's a cop-out, Monica, and you know it. The problem started months before I came to California— and it's about time you admitted it!"

"All right, let's both face the truth." She felt strong and in command and ten feet tall, although, iron- ically, she was still down on her knees. "When MacLaine Downes suddenly wrote that glowing recommendation—and I still don't know why he changed his mind—I made myself a promise. I swore that nothing would stop me from reaching my goals. Can you understand that?" Instead of an answer, there was only silence. He seemed to be struggling

with an odd sort of anger which was directed inwardly
. . . and not at her. She continued doggedly after a
moment, because she was almost blindly determined
to finish. "I intend to keep that promise, Jeff, in spite of
everything."

"Everything?"

"Yes—in spite of anything you do or say, even in
spite of anything I feel for you. Have I made myself
perfectly clear?"

"No, not quite." His frown slowly disappeared, but,
perversely, the tension mounted. "I don't understand
what you mean by 'anything I feel for you.' Go on,
Monica, tell me—perfectly and clearly."

Shocking herself, she felt relieved that she was
about to tell him the truth. "Don't laugh—it's really
very simple."

"I won't laugh, I promise you."

"I've learned to respect the reasons for your drive,
and I've always admired your intelligence. You're as
strong as I am, but you've shown me that you can be
gentle and vulnerable, too. I feel a 'healthy' amount of
passion for you," she said, smiling defiantly, "plus a
great deal of love. I know I should be certified a lunatic
for what I've just said, but those are some of the
reasons why I'm terribly attracted to you. No, go
ahead and laugh if you want, because I know it's
corny and mushy and ridiculously old-fashioned, isn't
it?"

"No, because I love you for the same reasons."

"Oh, really?"

"Don't smirk—I'm not joking."

She sat back and enjoyed the pleasure of finally telling him the truth. She felt wonderful. Oh, she knew it was only a momentary joy, but that didn't matter. She gazed at that handsome face for a few more seconds as if she were seeing it for the first time; then she plunged straight downward, back to earth. "So there's a lot of love in both of us, but we're still thousands of miles apart, in every way."

"But not quite so far apart, maybe, as we once were. It's rare when we both have the same ideas at the same time, so why don't we dump all our problems and differences for just one night? Why are you sitting over there with that funny look in your eyes? Why aren't you here, where you belong?"

"Because we've tried, but like oil and water, we just don't mix, Jeff. Oh, we've had our moments—great moments—but then you say something or I say something and the sparks start flying again."

"Perhaps because we've tried everything but this. . . ." He had left the low leather chair and was now kneeling on the floor in front of her. He moved closer, and without reaching to hold her, touched his mouth to hers. "Forget the thousands of miles between here and Washington, real or imaginary," he whispered, kissing one corner of her mouth and then slowly caressing the other side, "and, for once, meet me halfway."

"All the doubts will still be there in the morning."

"And now that I know how you feel, in the morning I think we'll find that most of them won't matter."

Now, when he finally reached to hold her, she

opened her arms, too, and captured him. He eased her back on the floor, pressing his body hotly to hers. It was perfectly clear to both of them that the time for reasoning was past.

They lay without moving for a long time while their lips came together, their arms around each other, bound by the thrill of discovery. He searched out every crevice of her mouth and she felt herself quivering with each strike of his tongue. He shuddered, too, when she returned the kiss just as deeply. They were clinging to each other, yet he demanded a stronger closeness. His thigh moved across the lower part of her body until he suddenly seized her legs in a vise between his. His chest and shoulders were pressing the breath from her. She couldn't even moan.

At last he moved his hands through her hair until he cupped her head, lifting it away from the hardness of the floor; she instantly arched her back, urging him to increase the hard, fast persuasion of his mouth. He was crushing her breasts and his touch was burning her skin, but for the first time in her life she was floating and spiraling with unknown passion—and she desperately wanted him to know it. Still, when he finally freed her just long enough to gasp a tiny bit of air, the only word she could whisper was his name, over and over. But that whisper told him everything.

The next morning, Monica awoke to the most beautiful sight she could ever imagine: Jeff turned, opened his eyes, and smiled at her. "I thought only angels wore halos," he murmured.

"That's right."

"Then why is your hair glowing like that?"

"Because the sun is shining on it."

"Can't be . . . the sun doesn't shine in the middle of the night."

"Darling, it's morning." She laughed softly.

"No," he moaned, sliding his arm under her head and pulling her over him so that she lay on his chest, "it's nighttime, and I'm just starting to peel away that silly top you're wearing and I've got you pinned under me on the floor. . . ."

"It's morning, and I'm not wearing anything, and we're in bed, not on the floor," she murmured, smiling against his skin.

"When did we get from the floor to the bed?"

"Sometime around dawn, when it suddenly started to get chilly. You carried me in here." She peeked up at him and teased, "Don't you remember anything that happened?"

"Only the important details," he assured her, closing his eyes to the sunshine, "but you could talk me into a refresher course. . . ."

"No, I don't think so."

"Why not?"

"Because you deliberately lied to me."

"About what?"

"About being tired," she murmured, licking the tight roundness of muscle just beneath his shoulder, remembering that he had taken her several stunning, beautiful times.

"Pure inspiration on my part." He wove his fingers

through the thickness of her hair and pressed her head down so that her open mouth was trapped against his body. "You're starting to inspire me again—and I don't want you to stop."

Her mouth was filled with the taste of him, but her hands were free to stroke at will, from the coarse black circles of hair on his chest to the dense downiness of his groin. She stopped only long enough to whisper, "Stop me from thinking about tomorrow, please. You promised. . . ."

"Don't talk crazy. Don't talk at all. . . ."

She rushed out of the shower, still soaking wet. "Jeff, I've just had a wonderful idea." Anything, anything to avoid the thought of *tomorrow* as long as possible!

He laughed, hiding his own anxiety, and flung back the sheet. "All right, come here."

"No—I'm talking about something else."

"Not interested," he said jokingly, dodging the droplets of water that sprang from her wet hair when she tossed her head in a mock show of impatience.

"Will you please be serious for a moment," she insisted.

"I am serious."

"Jeff, listen, I just remembered that today is Saturday."

"So?"

"So you could catch a plane back to Washington tomorrow, couldn't you?" *Please*, her eyes begged, *say yes. . . .*

"And still be at my desk Monday morning."

"And then we can spend the whole of today together."

"What's left of the day, you mean," he said, glancing at the small clock on her night table.

"It's only noon, so we do have the whole day."

"And night."

"And night, too."

"I know." He threw part of the sheet over her head and began to rub the dampness from her hair. "I'd already thought of it."

"Why didn't you say anything?"

"I wanted to wait and see if you really meant it when you swore that you would never let me go."

She wriggled out from under the sheet. "That's not fair! I said that in the heat of passion, but now it's broad daylight and . . ." And she was lying through her teeth.

"Does it make any difference," he wanted to know, as if he had read her mind, "if it's day or night?" He recaptured her in the folds of the sheet and briskly rubbed her down. *"I* can't leave *you,* darling, so I've already made up my mind not to go until tomorrow."

"But you were going to keep it a secret from me . . ."

"Only for a little while longer," he swore.

"Then you're forgiven," she whispered, loving the way he looked at her. But she decided to be firm, or they might never get out of bed. "I know exactly how we'll spend the day, so let's not waste another moment." She laughed and tugged at his arm with all her might. "Come on, get up!"

"So last night and this morning were just a waste of time, huh?" Standing, he brought her to him in an inescapable grip. "Answer me," he demanded, applying a little more pressure to the embrace.

"Anything *but,*" was the answer, just before she reached to kiss him. She welcomed the sensation of rubbing his body with hers, exploring it in a different way, while her arms remained locked around his neck. Amazing how wonderful she felt at this moment. . . .

The realization that he would be hers for only a few more hours stabbed through her like a knife. She had to stop thinking about that. "Darling, do you know we've never been alone together before . . . not for a whole day, I mean." She put her cheek on his chest and wound her arms tightly around his back. "I want to do ordinary things with you, everyday things, like just walking . . . and looking at other people and just *being* together. Do you know what I mean?"

"Of course," he whispered, very gently now, into her hair, "I know exactly what you mean. We'll spend the day doing anything you want. We could drive over to San Francisco, maybe, and just walk up and down the hills. If you like, we could stay there tonight, after a concert or supper in one of those great restaurants. . . ."

"Ah, no, that would be too civilized and distracting," she said, listening to the beat of his heart growing slower and more regular. "I think you should soak up a tiny bit of the wild, wild west. Something rustic and different."

"If you insist," he laughed, holding her at arm's length and trying not to concentrate on her lovely nakedness . . . but not quite succeeding. "Look, let me rush back to the hotel and I'll shower and shave and change my clothes."

"I suppose you didn't bring anything but perfectly tailored business things, huh?"

"Well, let's just say I didn't plan on roughing it through the countryside, anyway. Don't worry, I'll manage."

"At least don't wear one of your fancy ties."

"Okay, I promise. Where are we going, anyway?"

"To gaze upon history," she informed him unrelentingly.

"Couldn't you be a little more specific?"

"Specifically, forty-niner history—and I don't mean the football team." Then, because he still looked dubious, she soothed, "Don't look so unhappy. Trust me, you'll love it."

"I hope it won't be *too* educational. I might become so engrossed that I'll forget to kiss you, at least now and then."

"As if I'd let you forget," she whispered, moving back into his arms for one more sample of his mouth before she'd let him go.

"There—up ahead—take the turnoff to Sonora," Monica said, pointing. She settled back in her seat to glance sideways at Jeff. He had "managed" very well, she saw; the tweed jacket and wool slacks were just right for a clear, crisp day in the Gold Country. He hadn't worn a necktie and his shirt was opened comfortably at his throat. "You look nice," she told him boldly, cupping her hand around his shoulder. "Real nice."

The car swayed a fraction. "And you look beautiful, but I wish we weren't talking about clothes."

She laughed and matched his bantering tone. "If we weren't, we'd be arrested by the first local sheriff who saw us. Worse, because we'll soon be at the base of the Sierra, we'd probably freeze to death."

Monica herself was dressed comfortably in practical jeans, but she had added a soft silk blouse and, from experience, she had remembered to toss a warm velvet jacket in the backseat of the car. The jacket would also serve to dress up her casual appearance when they stopped to have dinner tonight. Monica already knew just where they'd stop.

Sonora was a small town, but it bustled with people, both native and tourist. It was the jumping-off point for the roads leading to the area's historic mining towns but it also featured its own old-time sites along the way. "Do we start the history lessons here?" Jeff asked.

"Yes, at one of my favorite places," Monica said, directing Jeff through a lovely park in the center of the town. They stopped at the foot of a hill a short distance away from the town's main square. A small early-California church blended into the topography; even the surrounding buildings, though also vintage, managed to dwarf the old religious house. On the side of the hill behind the church stood a simple chapel in poignant ruins. "What's that?" Jeff asked, shielding his eyes from the sun.

"The original place of worship built by the good padres before the main church was constructed. Want to go and explore?"

"Lead on," he said.

They took a winding rock path to the intriguing little chapel. "I read somewhere that the original doors were beautifully carved," she told him as they walked through the unprotected archway into the nave. Ten rows of pews, five on each side of the narrow aisle, were the only solid objects left in the chapel. All else, from the front doors to the roof, had perished with age. The sun beat down on a dirt floor. "It's a sad place," Jeff said, keeping his voice low and taking her hand in a tight clasp. "I don't mean just because it's in ruins, but I get a sad feeling standing here. Why is that, I wonder?"

"Ghosts, maybe?" she half-teased; however, unconsciously, she stepped closer to him. "It has a fascinating history, though."

"Does it?" He put his arm around her shoulder. "You seem to be well read on the place."

"I love western folklore," she admitted, smiling up at him. The sunlight felt so good and warm on her face, but not half as good as the light kiss he brushed against her cheek. "And I've read a lot of books on the history of early California."

"Just six months ago you were a bona fide easterner, and now you're a regular chamber of commerce for the entire state of California," he commented softly. Then he added, even more softly, "It doesn't take you long to fall in love once you've made up your mind, does it?"

She pulled away from him and began to stroll among the rows of dilapidated pews. "You're right, I did fall in love with the west immediately, but it didn't happen six months ago. It happened three years ago, when I first saw it."

Three years ago . . . when her husband was killed, he thought, but said nothing. The truth would come out sooner or later, and he wanted to let her tell the whole story at her own pace. "I didn't know you had been out here before," was all he said.

She nodded and then turned and smiled. The subject was abruptly changed. "Don't you notice anything strange about the size of these pews?"

"Yes," he answered, taking a closer look, "now that you mention it, I do. Each one seems long enough for just one person to kneel at." He walked to where she was standing. "Maybe I was just too busy looking at you . . . maybe that's why I didn't notice." He was glad that the dark cloud had passed from her lovely face. "Tell me why."

"This tiny chapel was built by ten monks for ten monks. It was done that way on purpose."

"And . . . ?"

"Only ten monks at a time were allowed to belong to their community."

"No more?"

"No," she replied, shaking her head and making her hair fly. "When one monk died, only then would another be allowed to take his place."

"Exclusive," he murmured.

"Hardly that," she laughed. "No, I think they just wanted to live in peace and simplicity."

"Well, they certainly found the right spot if that's what they wanted," he commented, realizing that he could hear only the chatter of birds. "Peace and simplicity. Does this place make you sad?"

"No."

"Then it doesn't seem so sad to me anymore, either."

"Be careful," she admonished, "or you'll start to fall in love with the wild west, too. Come on, let's go on or it'll be dark before we know it."

They continued to drive along the narrow old road until they came to Angels Camp. Here, at the very base of the Sierra Nevada, they viewed the silent sites where hordes of miners had once extracted precious metal from the deep shafts. The openings to these tunnels could still be seen, although the mines were now closed and abandoned. Here and there, a cluster of cabins attested to the fact that people had once lived and worked there, but now only a haunted silence prevailed. Except for the wind, of course. It howled and screamed its way down the steep slopes of the omnipotent white-crowned mountains. "Dramatic, isn't it?" Monica murmured.

Jeff nodded. "Let's stop for a moment."

"Fine."

"Seems cold out there. Why don't you wait in the car while I have a look around?"

"I have my jacket, so I won't be cold."

He climbed out of the car and walked a few paces away. With the wind tearing at his clothes and hair, he stopped and looked around. She followed, but kept quiet because she wanted him to experience the full impact of the landscape without disturbance. Finally, his words cut into the hypnotic cadence of the wind. "How could they live here?" he said wonderingly, nodding toward the deserted mining town not too far in the distance. Only a few ramshackle buildings remained, leaning crazily, with empty windows and detached slats flying in the wind. "How did people survive with the constant wind and the storms and the cold and the loneliness?"

"Greed, I suppose. Maybe stubbornness. Obsession." It was suddenly becoming very cold. She went to stand close to him, leaning on him for protection against the blasts of air. "Probably they believed that any sacrifice was worth it."

"But for *what*, for God's sake?"

"Gold, the brass ring, easy living in the big cities, power—I don't know." She was starting to shiver, but it wasn't from the cold. "I suppose loneliness is a small price to pay to reach a goal or a dream."

She gazed quickly at Jeff and then turned her face to the mountain. So, once again, here she was involved with a man who wanted to reach a summit! That precise ambition had already brought tragedy into her life, and Jeff MacKennon was much more ambitious than her husband had been. There was a marked difference, however, between the two relationships— one that she had better not forget, she warned herself. She had married Jim Bloomquist knowing full well that his career was the paramount interest in his life, but Jeff MacKennon didn't belong to her . . . and it mattered very little that, sometime near dawn, they had both alluded to love. At this stage of the game, she had no right to meddle with his obsession. . . .

Suddenly overcome by the sadness of it all, Monica said shakily, "It's so cold!"

He turned to cradle her in his arms. "Is it the winds, Monica, or the ghosts?"

She summoned her common sense. "Holly swears that I look spooked sometimes, but I think her imagination is working overtime." She nuzzled her cheek against his arm. "No, darling, I'm not a believer in ghost stories."

She couldn't see his skeptical smile. "Then you're shivering from the cold, so let's get back to the car."

Protected from the elements and comfortable again in the car, he held her hands, rubbing them between his palms. "Hey, I thought I was supposed to be the tenderfoot," he gently teased.

"I'll be fine in a moment."

"Monica, look at me."

All the gentleness she had ever yearned for was alive in his eyes. "I'm all right, really, don't worry."

"I *am* worried, but it's because I've failed you, in an awful way, haven't I?"

"Failed? No, Jeff, never. . . ."

"Yes, I have. I've failed because I couldn't drive all the doubts away." He wrapped his arms around her and buried her head on his chest. "But we have hours and hours yet, together."

But nothing will change, she wanted to scream; instead, she forced her teeth to stop chattering, and tried to laugh. "You know something, I think I'm just hungry, that's all."

He accepted her excuse. "You're a real brat, aren't you? Here I am, scouring my soul, and all you think about is a hamburger."

"I'm a very basic kind of person," she ad-libbed quickly, before the dark mood returned.

"Then I'd better get you back to civilization as soon as possible." He peered up and down the desolate road. "By the way, which way *is* civilization?"

"That way," she said, pointing straight ahead. "We'll go on to Columbia."

"It's very civilized, I hope."

"Very. Come on, trust me."

"All right, we'll see!" He turned and started the motor. "But just in case some ghost decides to hitch a ride—why don't you sit very close to me, and that way we'll be sure to leave it behind."

6

~oooooooooo~

By the time they arrived in the restored gold-rush town of Columbia, Monica felt warm and sane again. The sun was just beginning to slant behind the mountains and the little hamlet looked charming in the early-eveing glow, with gaslights flickering in the streets and in the shops.

The tiny city looked like a museum piece, a picture postcard quite different from the melancholy scenario of the ghostly mining towns on its borders. She looked at Jeff and said, "See, I promised you civilization, didn't I?"

"And maybe something a bit more exotic than hamburgers?" he begged, glad to see her in good spirits again.

"Oh, I assure you, you won't have to rough it for supper here."

"Good—I didn't want to have to go up in those mountains and shoot us a bear, or something equally primitive!"

She smiled at the image of Jeff MacKennon hunting for his supper in the Sierra Nevada. "Why don't you park the car here, and then we can walk to the Gold Dust Hotel. It's a tiny town and it'll take us only a few minutes to get there."

"Sure you won't be cold?" he asked, locating and pulling into a parking place.

"No, not if you hold me close while we walk."

They strolled slowly along the carefully preserved wooden sidewalks, as much enthralled with the nearness of each other as by the sights of the quaint town. Curio shops sold souvenirs and the narrow streets were dotted with "saloons" and "emporiums."

"The whole place looks like a western movie set," Jeff said in jest.

"Don't be cynical," Monica chided, rubbing her cheek on his shoulder, "and use your imagination. Get into the spirit of the old west!"

They passed a tiny shop that specialized in photographing tourists in mid-nineteenth-century costumes. A man and woman were having their picture taken— he as a mustachioed card shark and she as a dancehall floozy—and Jeff and Monica stopped to watch. The "card shark" looked somewhat embarrassed about the whole thing, but the "floozy" was having a ball posing as a shady lady, pulling at her already deep-cut bodice and sprucing up her garish array of gaudy feathers.

"You know," Jeff whispered in Monica's ear,

"you'd look great in that outift. Why don't you get into the spirit of the old west and have your picture taken in that dress?"

"And I suppose you'd show it to everybody in Washington, wouldn't you?"

"You bet I would."

"Jeff MacKennon, you're a louse!" She tugged at his arm, pulling him away from the photographer's shop. "Anyway, I don't look good in feathers," she laughed, letting him clasp her hand again, "and I'm really very hungry."

A few minutes later they reached the facade of the lovely old building bearing the legend "Gold Dust Hotel—1859." It was small, but it was filled with a glow and warmth that reached outside to induce the passerby to come inside. Monica preceded Jeff into a lobby containing assorted pieces of velvet period furnutire, and then they stepped across a polished, aged wooden floor to the entrance of the dining room. "I feel as if I've gone back in time," he said.

"Wait until you see the dining room," she assured him.

They were seated next to a window overlooking the narrow "main street." The room wasn't large and could serve only a handful of people, but the tables had been situated in an artful way so that the feeling was one of privacy and coziness. On each table stood a little vase of mountain flowers, and the cloths beneath were pristine white and reached to the floor. The walls were covered with rose damask wallpaper. Ladies and gentlemen of the last century, captured

forever in their Sunday best, gazed down from faded
rotogravure prints, and tawny mirrors in fan-shaped
frames reflected the fluttering waves of gaslight lamps.
A cheery fire burned under a hand-carved mantelpiece along one end of the room. A picturesque bar
spanned the length of the opposite wall, featuring
above it the obligatory painting of a reclining naked
beauty, rosy pink and well-endowed, holding aloft a
cluster of ruby-red grapes. In short, the room was a
perfect blend of the sentimental and the nostalgic—
and it was marvelous.

"If the food is half as good as the atmosphere," Jeff
said, "I think I'm going to enjoy this place very much."

Monica's eyes sparkled. "Oh, yes, I can vouch for
the quality of the cuisine. The Gold Dust Hotel boasts
a cordon bleu chef in its kitchen."

"You're putting me on."

"Would I do that to you? Sit and relax," she said,
"and prepare yourself for a superb gastronomical
experience."

The meal, served in unhurried, easy stages, was a
dream: thin slices of ham and figs as an appetizer; veal
brushed with lemon for an entrée; fresh garden straw-
berries and wedges of soft cheese for dessert. Each
course was accompanied by an appropriate California
wine, culminating with the serving of a local port to
finish the fabulous meal. By the time coffee was
brought to the table, both Jeff and Monica were in a
content but reflective mood. "What are you thinking?" she asked.

"That this was wonderful," he answered, waving

his hand over an assortment of imaginary dishes, ". . . but only because I could look across the table and see you."

"Thank you . . . that was a beautiful thing to say. But I have a feeling you were thinking about something else."

"Not really." He smiled, brushing away her idea.

"Jeff, tell me something."

"If I can."

"Why did you turn down the White House job?" She rushed to add, "Forgive me for being inquisitive, but I simply can't believe you did such a thing."

"It was nothing mysterious, Monica. I received the offer, I thought about it, and then I decided I didn't want a political appointment, that's all."

"But why, all of a sudden . . ."

"Why didn't I stop to consider the consequences before?" he finished the thought for her.

"Yes, that's exactly what I was wondering."

"Maybe I have never given myself the breathing space to stop and sort it out." He closed his eyes for a second and then reached to grasp her hand. "Darling, maybe I suddenly realized that it was dangerous to be *too* ambitious—for the wrong reasons. I was suddenly within reach of the top, but it was too soon. I'm still young enough—I have plenty of time to learn a great deal more." The hold on her hand tightened perceptibly. "I want to make my own political mistakes and get credit for my own successes, so I've been considering something else."

"What, Jeff? Please tell me."

"I've been considering—sometime in the future—running for an elective office."

He had finally managed to shock her into total speechlessness. He flexed his fingers around her hand, and then murmured, "Why are you so surprised? Don't you think I have ideals and convictions like everybody else?"

"Don't be harsh, Jeff, of course I know that," she answered finally, "but I assumed, rashly, perhaps, that you had different goals in mind."

"Money and power and prestige, for instance?"

She lowered her eyes, groping desperately for the right words. She finally opted for complete honesty. "I admit I've been guilty of suspecting you of having the worst possible motives, all right. But that was because you made me believe that you craved money and power above everything. I'm glad I was wrong. I'm very sorry I never considered the fact that there was a part of you that you wanted to keep private and hidden. Please don't hate me for being so shallow and blind."

"Hate you?" He sounded incredulous. He started to bring her captured hand to his mouth, but suddenly became aware of others in the room. Several tables were occupied, and although an aura of privacy surrounded the guests, it was still a public place. "If we can't be alone in the next few minutes, Monica, I think I'll go a little crazy."

She believed him; she was seized with the same insane impulse. "There's a small sitting room in the lobby. . . ."

"Will they serve some brandy there?"

"Yes, I think so."

The room, hardly more than a secluded alcove, provided a perfect refuge for them. The only light came from the glow of the fireplace, it was quiet, and it would remain empty—except for Monica and Jeff—because the waiter who brought in the brandies left with a large tip in his pocket.

Monica immediately moved to be caught in Jeff's arms. They clung to each other, swaying a little, eyes closed, heads pressed tightly together. They didn't exchange a kiss; they simply held on to each other with all their strength. She felt his breath on her throat when he whispered, "Ask me again if I hate you."

"I wouldn't blame you . . . I've given you enough cause," she said with a soft moan, burying her face deeper into his shoulder. "But I don't want to think about the past tonight."

"When, then?"

Because his mouth was pressed into her hair, she couldn't quite hear the words and thought she had misunderstood. "What . . . ?"

"I asked you, when will you face the past—your past—and share it with me? I need to know you, Monica, and everything that's happened to you until that moment when I first saw you. If I don't know your past, how will I be able to fight off the ghosts and the doubts? Help me, darling."

They stepped apart and gazed at each other. "So much has happened to me . . ." she murmured, turning away slightly.

The brandies had been set on a low table near the

fireplace. She picked up one of the snifters and gazed at the firelight filtering through the liquid within. "It's hard to talk about yourself. Do you know what I mean? Where do I begin, for instance?"

He reached for the other brandy and drank. "Begin by telling me why you've never practiced law. It's tough to get through law school, and yet you did it and then never used your degree. Why, Monica?"

She sat down on the only other piece of furniture in the alcove, a Victorian side chair framed in curlicued rosewood with a matching footstool. "I'll have to tell you about Jim, then."

"Yes, if it doesn't hurt too much to talk about your husband."

"Not too much, really, not anymore." She concentrated her gaze once again on the brandy while she attempted to conjure up an image of James Madison Bloomquist III, the man who had been her husband—for a very short time. The image, however, remained elusive. "Funny, I can't remember exactly what he looked like even though I had known him most of my life before our marriage. We came from families that had known each other for ages, we went to school together, and then we went to law school together. Then, afterward, our families decided we should spend our lives together, too. Why not, since on paper, at least, the union should have been perfect." She smiled cynically, remembering the reality of her marriage. "Jim had no trouble receiving an appointment in the Attorney General's office—his own brilliance coupled with his family connections made it a sure thing—but I, meanwhile, let myself be convinced that I should be spending my time choosing patterns for the silver and china and crystal instead of practicing law. You don't know how much time a person can waste doing such stupid things!" she murmured, staring into the fire. "But it was my own fault—I allowed it to happen to me."

"Your father . . . ?"

"Oh, he was concerned about my happiness, but he never, not for an instant, pressured me into the marriage."

"Then why did you go ahead with it? The marriage, I mean? You, who can be so stubborn!"

"I decided I was going to be a wife, and I stubbornly insisted I was going to be a perfect Washingtonian wife, don't you see?"

"Yes," he murmured, "I see, all right. But you were telling me about your father."

"My mother died when I was young, so my father became very protective. He was especially hopeful that I would marry Jim because he'd had a hand in guiding his career and he knew that Jim would provide for me, quite comfortably, for the rest of my life. Later . . . well, my father's still indulging me, but now he's very scrupulous about letting me make my own decisions. No, I never blamed him for what happened. Thinking back," she continued, "I can't blame Jim, either, because by that time he was as deeply trapped in the situation as I was."

Monica closed her eyes for a second; Jeff remained very still, letting her wander into the past step by step. "We even postponed the wedding a few times when our families suggested we wait for the 'proper' Georgetown town house—white shutters inside, black shutters outside, five steps up from the street, all-brick facade, small courtyard in the back with a miniature garden—you know the setup." Out of the corner of her eye she saw him nod; then she took a deep sip from her glass. "But neither of us bothered to protest the delay, because he had his work and his aspirations to occupy his mind, and I . . ." She stopped, sorting her thoughts, wanting to be painfully candid. "He had enough ambition for both of us and I felt defeated, I suppose."

In the shadows, Jeff went to the fireplace and carefully set his glass on the mantelpiece. If Monica had been looking at his face, she would have been astounded by the expression in his eyes. But the past had completely captured her mind and her gaze seemed to be focused at the bottom of the empty snifter in her hand. "Anyway, by this time, neither of us was in a rush to get married."

"A relationship doesn't start when the preacher reads from the Good Book or when the guests begin drinking the champagne," he reminded her, turning to watch her and gently coaxing her memory. "You two must have had some sort of relationship going at this time. Love . . . sex . . . or both?"

Her mouth curved. "Oh, we loved each other out of habit. Sex? Once in a while." The look in her eyes left no doubt that it had been devoid of any excitement or passion. Unconsciously her glance turned to Jeff; guiltily she looked away quickly. "It wasn't his fault and it wasn't mine. The chemistry just wasn't there. Anyway, *first* we signed the lease on the town house and then we were married. It was a June ceremony in my father's garden. It was deliberately exclusive, just the close family members—no big society thing. It was the 'ideal' wedding between a somber judge's daughter and a brilliant young lawyer who was blazing his way to the top. Then we settled down . . . and he went to work *every* day and traveled a great deal and I stayed at home going through the motions of being a homemaker in an empty house. Now and then I toyed with the idea of joining a law firm, but mostly I . . ." She set the glass down on the floor with a hand that wasn't too steady. "Jim wasn't supportive, but he wasn't negative, either, about my on-again, off-again plans to go to work. We didn't need the money, after all, and he felt that it was a decision I should make on my own. He was right about that, at least."

Jeff stirred. There was something tense, almost angry about the set of his shoulders. His question, when it finally came, was slightly sharp. "So why didn't you begin to practice law? What stopped you from using all your brains and training and talent, for God's sake?"

"Something very prosaic and yet very special. Something totally unexpected," she replied with a sad smile. "I found out that I was pregnant."

He smothered the curse in time, angry now only with himself. "And you wanted the baby?"

"How could I not want my own child?" She was pensive. "I might have wished for more time to myself, to plan for children in the future, but it was still my baby. Jim was in Mexico City on government business and he called that evening—after I had gone to the doctor and gotten the test results—to tell me that he wouldn't be coming home. Instead, he was being sent to South America on some fact-finding mission. He would only be gone five days, he told me, and then he would return directly to Washington. I didn't want to tell him that I was pregnant—not like that, not on the phone—so I decided to wait until he came home. But his plane crashed on the journey back to the States and I never had the chance to tell him, you see."

"And the baby?"

"I miscarried two days after Jim was killed."

Startled, Monica suddenly realized that Jeff was half-kneeling, half-sitting on the footstool in front of her, grasping her hands in his as tightly as he could without crushing her fingers. He looked so troubled that she bent to comfort him, returning the pressure of his grasp. "Darling, it's all right," she whispered, "the pain is all gone, don't worry."

"But it must have been awful for you." His voice was compassionate.

If she nodded at all, it was scarcely noticeable. "But I got over it. When I felt stronger and healthier, I closed the town house and took a long vacation in California. I fell hopelessly in love with it. When I returned to Washington, I was determined to find some sort of interesting work—but I vowed I would return to the west someday. And the rest is history." She laughed lightly.

"And you kept your vow and returned," he stated, "and you're very happy here."

"And I never brood about the past," she assured him, brushing a kiss across his cheek. "I suppose a psychologist would insist that I chose working with youngsters because of some deep maternal complex that I had to fulfill, but I don't worry about it because if it's true, at least I'm compensating in a worthwhile, healthy way, wouldn't you agree?"

"Sure." But he was concentrating on another matter, one that was more immediate. "You've done a beautiful job coming to grips with your past, darling, but the question is . . . how will you compensate for what's happening to us?" He took her face and brought it very close to his. "How are you going to deal with the clash between your determination and my ambition?"

Her first instinct was to lash out and remind him that the problem was *theirs*, and not hers alone, but in the next instant she realized that he had gotten to the core of the dilemma: he had never denied his ambitions and he would never change, so ultimately the choice must be hers. It would be a wrenching decision, but it had to be made. However, not now, she pleaded with herself . . . not so soon. They were sharing something too lovely, too precious to shatter. Her hand crept up to his mouth and her fingertips softly sealed his lips. "Don't ask me any more questions tonight, or you'll bring back the ghosts."

He kissed her fingers and then freed his mouth. "Then I won't, I promise."

They sat close together for a long while. It was Jeff who first heard the intrusive tapping against the weather-beaten windows. "It must be the rain."

She knew better. "No, it's the wind rushing down from the mountains."

"Then it must be very cold outside."

"Absolutely."

"So why should we leave this warm place?"

"We shouldn't," she whispered. "Do you think the hotel might have a room for us? I think there are only three or four guest rooms, unfortunately."

"I don't know why, but I think we're going to be in luck." He stood and pulled her up with him. "Let's find out."

The reservation clerk smiled at them from behind her gold-rimmed granny glasses. "Did you enjoy your supper?"

"Yes, very much," Jeff assured the cheerful woman. "Actually, we enjoyed our visit so much that we don't want to leave. You wouldn't by chance have a room that you could let us have for the night, would you?"

"Oh, I'm so sorry, but our guest rooms have all been reserved," the woman told him, sighing with regret. "If only you'd called in advance."

"I did, earlier today," Monica replied, smiling at the woman, "and you told me that your loveliest room just happened to be available, as a matter of fact."

"Oh, are you Miss Monica Lewis?"

"That's right."

After they had signed the guest register, the smiling woman handed Jeff the key to their room. He took Monica by the hand and they began to climb the beautiful wooden staircase to the second floor. When they reached the top of the stairs, he turned and said,

"I told you I had the feeling we'd be in luck tonight, didn't I?"

It was the kind of room where the drapes matched the bedspread. Little toss pillows, tucked into the backs and sides of turn-of-the-century love seats, featured the same flowery design which highlighted the wallpaper. A fire sparked and crackled in the grate, caught in the downdraft of the howling wind outside. "This room's a picture book come to life!" Monica twirled in a semicircle. "Isn't it marvelous?"

"Yeah, but it also makes me feel like the proverbial bull in a china shop. How did men make themselves comfortable in those days without splintering the furniture?"

She caught him around the waist and squeezed a little. "They took off their boots and unslung their gunbelts and moved very slowly and sensually."

"Not in the westerns I've seen!" he said emphatically, letting her go on holding him. "I thought they were gentle only with their horses." He knew that she was deliberately pretending; perhaps tomorrow would never come if he also pretended. Somehow, he kept the tension out of his voice. "By the way, I like the way you managed to get us this room." He wound his arms around her shoulders and held her very close to him. "Did you also mastermind that windstorm outside?"

"I didn't have to, because I knew I could rely on good old mother nature to do her thing. Happy?"

"More than just happy."

"Tell me how you feel."

"Using plain, ordinary words?"

"That's the best way, isn't it?"

"Not always." Easing her toward the bed, he leaned back on it and began slowly to pull her down on top of him. "Sometimes this way is better, holding you and feeling you growing soft and wonderful. Body language, I think it's called."

She let her body mold to his. "I want to hear you talk about it."

"About how I'm going to make love to you," he whispered, "or how I love you?"

She was quiet for a moment, barely breathing. "Both . . . if that's what you want."

"I want both, but I think I'd better start with plain, ordinary words." He held her head down on his shoulder so that she couldn't turn to look at him. "I love you."

She waited awhile, relishing the meaning of those three words, and then she broke his grip and forced her head up. The windows were rattling so hard that it sounded as if a fist were banging on them. "And I love you."

There was something moody and haunted about his whisper. "I don't want to think anymore, Monica. I'm tired of thinking in circles about you and me. I want to forget that anything else exists in this world but you and me. . . ."

She gazed at his face in the semidarkness, as if she yearned to engrave the features in her mind forever, and then she closed her eyes. "Nothing else exists but this," she insisted, feeling with her lips until she found his eyes to kiss them, "and this," she said, finding his mouth, "and this," she whispered as she slowly loosened his clothes and twisted over him. "Talk to me about this. . . ."

The feverish words reached her in alluring waves, faint and then strong, as he breathed his pleas and desires. She waited a second or two each time before placing her warm mouth down the length of his body, provoking both of them, inciting the flames. Soon the words died and he could only groan. But he suddenly convulsed and leaned to grab hold of her. Then he had her pinned beneath him, and it was her turn to moan and to plead and to talk about love and unbearable desire. He fed the flames without teasing her, hypnotically letting the heat consume them long into the night.

They were both in a strange state in the morning, sleepy and groggy and yet nervously sensitive. When they walked down the stairs to the foyer of the hotel, the aromas from the dining room made Monica realize that she had no appetite. At any other time, the combination of crisp bacon and homemade biscuits would have made her mouth water, but not today. Jeff spoke first. "You should have something, darling. Coffee or juice, at least."

"What about you?"

"I might manage a cup of coffee."

"Coffee for me, too. Maybe we could have it here in the foyer."

So breakfast turned out to be a fast cup of coffee for both of them. Later, swaying with the movement of the car going at top speed on the highway back to

Sacramento, she began to feel a little light-headed. *Stop it,* she told herself; it's only nerves. Nerves and a terrible sadness. Sadness because he would be gone in a few hours. "What time does your plane leave?"

"Noon."

The clock on the dashboard read nine-forty-five. "Are you turning in the car at your hotel?"

"Yes, but first I'll leave you at your apartment."

She must have a few extra precious moments with him somehow. "Then I'll drive you in my car to the airport."

"I could take a cab from the hotel."

"No, I want to be with you as long as possible."

"That's what I'd hoped you'd say."

She glanced at him. He looked grim and unhappy. She moved closer to him. "Smile a little—or I might begin to suspect that I'm a lousy lover."

That ridiculous statement caused a slight upward curve along the edge of his mouth. "Don't talk crazy."

"At least I got you to stop frowning." She snuggled closer, hating to be even a fraction away from him, trying desperately, at the same time, to distract him. "Just out of curiosity, how would you rate me?"

"Off the charts."

"Top or bottom?"

His smile was a little broader now. "I'll keep you guessing." However, the frown quickly returned. "I love you, Monica. I love you and I'm *very ambitious,* remember?"

"Don't do this to us," she said pleadingly, "not at the last moment."

"I'm so ambitious that I'm leaving you to go back to

161

Washington instead of turning this car around and letting everything else go to hell for the next few days."

A spasm went through her body and she clutched at his shoulder. "Oh, darling, please, don't. . . ."

They were on the outskirts of Sacramento now and they didn't say another word to each other for the rest of the ride.

The elevator taking them to the boarding gate seemed to be moving at extraordinary speed. Everything seemed to be moving or happening too fast this morning, Monica realized. Too fast—too soon—too unreal. Jeff was leaning on the railing, a step behind her, but pressed very close to her. "Smile, or people will think *I* was a lousy lover last night," he whispered so that only she could hear.

The intimate little joke brought back the light-headedness, but she fought it, in desperation. "Don't, Jeff—because I think I'm going to cry and I swore I'd never let you see me do that."

They had reached the upper level of the air terminal and they began to walk down the esplanade housing the many departure gates. "Don't cry, just tell me you love me."

She barely choked back a sob. "I love you. . . ."

He suddenly reached to catch her arm. "You make it sound so sad, Monica." He searched her face and then murmured, "What you really mean is good-bye, isn't it?"

"Yes."

"I won't let it be good-bye."

A totally impersonal voice on an intercom system called Jeff's name, instructing him to proceed to Gate Ten or to pick up any white service telephone in the boarding area. Jeff ignored it. "Funny, isn't it?" he said, staring at Monica without any humor at all in his dark eyes. "Other people say 'I love you' and it's the beginning, it means they have to be together, but with us it only means good-bye."

"Other people, yes, but *we* knew it would be impossible, right from the start."

"That's what *you've* been thinking all along, not me." Without waiting for her answer, he walked away. She was so intent on keeping up with his long steps that she stumbled when he stopped altogether. "The only thing that matters now is," he declared, "do you want to be with me?"

"For God's sake, Jeff, what do you think?"

"Then there's only one answer." He stopped her protest with a curt, angry shake of his head. "Look, Monica, I'm going to level with you. The next few weeks will be tough for me, job-wise. Never mind that my whole future is up in the air because I refused that White House position—I'm still the funding director of a very large agency and I'm still responsible for the functioning of my department. I have a full schedule—conferences, projects, planning, budget meetings. . . ."

As she listened to him recite *his* schedule and *his* career problems and *his* responsibilities, she felt the old resentment building and swelling. "I know," she snapped, rushing to catch up to him as he began to walk again, "you're a very important person. But exactly what are you trying to tell me?"

"That I'm not about to be logging a whole lot of miles between coasts in the near future on personal business."

"I didn't expect you to do that, Jeff!"

An insistent air attendant broke into whatever Jeff was about to say. "Excuse me, sir. Are you Mr. Jeff MacKennon?"

"Yes."

"We've been paging you, sir," the attendant said with just the right amount of snap to his voice that he sounded efficient and not rude. "Flight Five to Washington, D.C.," he said, indicating over his shoulder the gleaming silver plane beyond the thick glass window, "is scheduled for immediate departure. You'd better board now, sir. May I have your ticket?"

Jeff handed it over and the attendant fussed with it. Meanwhile, Jeff turned to stare at Monica; it was a look of anger mixed with mute supplication. She knew what was going on in his mind, but she fought against the compulsion to give in to it. This was no time to weaken. The only thing left to do was to make the break as cleanly as possible.

Meanwhile, the attendant finished mutilating Jeff's ticket. "You're all set now, Mr. MacKennon. Please follow that ramp"—he pointed to the left with a stern finger—"to the first-class compartment. Have a nice trip, sir."

Her dizziness had increased and Monica was feeling positively ill. "Good-bye, Jeff."

But he didn't move. "I don't have to take this flight, you know."

"It won't be any easier to say good-bye tomorrow," she replied.

The attendant, still standing nearby, issued a warning. "Mr. MacKennon, please, we really can't hold the plane any longer."

Jeff cut the man short with a swift, frigid look. "We don't have to say good-bye tomorrow, Monica, or at any other time. We can go back to your apartment and draft a letter of resignation. We can put it on your department supervisor's desk in the morning, and we can be in Washington tomorrow night." He gave a quick look around. "I can call my secretary right now and tell her to cancel my appointments for tomorrow."

"Don't bother," she said in a dead, flat voice, "because I'm not going to Washington with you, tomorrow or at any other time."

He knew she meant it. Looking deeply into her eyes, there was no way he could mistake her stubborn resolve to remain. "All right, then. I've kept this plane waiting long enough." He started to move away, but the irony and sarcasm of his last words reached her clearly. "Let's keep in touch, anyway. But if you have any trouble reaching me in the next few days, keep in mind that I'll be spending most of my time supervising the allocations committee while it reviews your case."

7

The days following Jeff's departure were horrible for Monica. Finally, her moodiness and silence drove Holly up the wall. "It might help a little if you talked about what's making you quietly nuts, you know, Monica," urged Holly.

"There's nothing to talk about," Monica mumbled, staring at some papers on her desk, "and until we hear from Washington, we'd better concentrate on other business in this office, don't you think?"

"Okay, don't snap my head off," Holly retaliated, but not too harshly. "I thought it might do you good to blow off some steam," she suggested, "so that you won't be wasting your time around here."

"What do you mean?"

"You've been reading and rereading that same paragraph all morning, my friend."

Monica finally looked up. "It's that obvious, huh?"

"It sure is."

Giving the papers a push, Monica sighed. "Look, I'm sorry, Holly, but I meant it when I said there's nothing to discuss. It's all over between Jeff Mac-Kennon and me. That's an overstatement, really. Actually, it never really began. Just say it was lovely while it lasted."

Holly was quick to fill in the missing pieces, despite Monica's unembellished words. "I assume that your being *here* and his being *there* had everything to do with the breakup; am I right?"

"Oh, there were one or two other problems involved," Monica dryly conceded, "like the stark truth that I have a career which doesn't happen to coincide with Mr. MacKennon's 'Great Plan' for his own future."

"And yet," Holly summarized sagely, "what happens to your career in the future depends on Mr. MacKennon's ability to get you the funding, doesn't it?"

"Not really," Monica declared. "I'll go on, with or without the funding."

"You know, Monica," Holly murmured, "sometimes it's not healthy to be too stubborn."

"You're sounding like an oracle again, Holly." Monica gazed with suspicion at her closest friend. "I know that tone of voice, and it usually means you're hiding something—so tell me what it is."

"Not until you swear to me that you're all right."

"Holly—come on, *give.*"

"Well, a person might think she has answers

for everything, but sometimes unexpected things happen. . . ."

"Like what?" Monica was on the verge of losing her temper, but she stopped herself from lashing out at Holly. "What do you mean by 'unexpected things'? Don't be afraid—tell me!"

"Okay," Holly said, with more worry than temper showing in her voice, "I'll come clean." She went to her desk, picked up a white business-length envelope, and slapped it down in front of Monica. "This came by special courier while you were out on an errand. I guess I just wanted to be sure your nerves were strong enough to take another shock before I gave it to you, that's all. I don't know what's in that letter, of course, but I do know it's from Jeff MacKennon and it looks very official."

Holly was right; the letter *did* look official. Monica carefully scanned the surface of the envelope, but she didn't touch it. The bond of the paper appeared forbiddingly expensive, and so did the embossed lettering in the upper left-hand corner stating Jeff's full name—Jeffrey Thomas MacKennon—and his full title at the Department of Education.

Although Holly was breathing down her neck, Monica took her time and let Jeff's name slide through her mind for a few seconds because the sight of it—so formal in dark blue letters—suddenly sent a shiver through her body. To stop the strange reaction from reaching Holly's eyes, Monica quickly ripped open the envelope. Her gaze darted from the letterhead to the text, and then swiftly ran down the terse, short message: "Dear Ms. Lewis: I have presented my report regarding your request for emergency funds to my agency's budget allocations committee. Although it seems highly probable that the decision will be in your favor, I think you should know that it will take longer to reach a final decision than I had originally anticipated. If you hope to have the money in time to implement your student work-pay program this summer, I suggest that you come to Washington as soon as possible and personally reinforce your request for immediate funding. Sincerely . . ."

Monica looked hard at the signature. It was signed in bold strokes, "Jeffrey T. MacKennon"—and there was no personal postscript beneath it. She handed the letter to Holly without comment; meanwhile, her mind was working furiously. What was this, another MacKennon ploy? Was it just her imagination, or was there an implied threat in the terse message? Come to Washington, or endanger the funding? Was he telling her the truth—or was he playing games with her—*again?*

The letter was dangling from Holly's fingers. "This looks serious, Monica. What are you going to do?"

Monica was already a step ahead of Holly. "What else can I do but jump when the director of funding for the Department of Education gives an order?" Still, she showed her uncertainty by hedging. "Do you think I'd have a problem with our department supervisor? Would he sanction the cost of a trip to Washington, I mean?"

"Are you joking?" Holly laughed somewhat hysterically and let the letter fall out of her hands. "To get the necessary money for the summer programs, I think our department's top brass would personally escort you to the airport and see you off with kisses, flowers and a marching band!" But she was too nervous to keep up with the joke. "Monica, the question is . . . do you want to face Jeff MacKennon again? What do *you* want to do?"

"Me?" Monica stroked the letter flat and then laid her palms over it, obscuring what was written on it. "I want to go to Washington and face Jeff MacKennon and his damned agency—and come back a winner."

The polished surface of the long mahogany conference table was dotted with only a few articles—white memo pads, china cups and saucers, a water carafe and crystal glasses—so Monica was able to look down its length and see Jeff's face reflected there clearly. She was glad; otherwise, seated as he was at the far end of the table, she would have been forced to twist and bend to catch a glimpse of him—and she didn't want to do that.

Monica was certain that he had intentionally placed himself at a distance from her for two days now. They had exchanged only polite, formal words; she was glad about that, too. "You did the smart thing coming to Washington," were the first words he'd said to her yesterday when she entered the conference room in the Capitol Building. Then, as an afterthought, he'd said, "It's good to see you, Monica."

She had replied with the same detachment. "I hope you're right about my appearance before the committee being so important, Jeff." The omission of a personal query was quite deliberate. "My supervisor will be very upset if this trip turns out to be an expense that wasn't really necessary."

His reply was swift and sharp: "Your supervisor—and you—will be more upset if the funding doesn't come through until *after* the summer." Then the meeting was called to order and he had shown her to her seat; the only words they'd addressed to each other after that were strictly business.

Yesterday's questioning by the members of the allocations committee had seemed endless, and Monica had gone wearily to her father's house at the close of the session, wanting only to fall into bed. She had barely spoken to Judge Lewis since her arrival in Washington forty-eight hours earlier, and she had awakened this morning to find some affectionate fatherly words scrawled on a notepad by her coffee cup in the sun-splashed breakfast room. Ending the cheerful little note was a parental admonition: ". . . Barring only a final call to Judgment Day by the Almighty, I'll expect you to have supper with me tonight, my dearest daughter. Understood?"

Now, in the sedate conference room, Monica smiled as she recalled her father's command—and she nearly missed a question directed to her by a committee member. She pulled her thoughts together and answered as concisely as possible. "I would say that unless my department receives the funds as soon as possible, yes, the entire program will be in danger of collapse by next year."

Whatever doubts Monica might have had prior to yesterday's session about the necessity of appearing in person to guarantee the immediate issue of funds had quickly been squashed. Jeff hadn't misled her after all, and she had done him an injustice by believing that he was merely playing a cruel hoax by pressuring her to come to Washington under false pretenses. In fact, she had listened with surprise and growing gratitude this morning as he continually made positive and helpful remarks concerning her program. Of course, he *had* kept his eyes averted from hers and she hadn't looked directly at him, either, but she honestly intended to remedy that situation as soon as this morning's session ended. Whatever the outcome of the meeting, she owed him a great deal. But she had noticed, indeed, that every time she'd answered a question this morning, she had been rewarded with a sympathetic nodding of heads and a round of consenting smiles from the members of the committee. *It looks good,* she told herself, mentally crossing her fingers.

The conference-room door suddenly opened and MacLaine Downes strolled in. Nobody seemed surprised by his presence but Monica. He nodded amiably to the members of the committee, saving a broad smile for Jeff. "Mind if I sit for a while and listen to the reports?" MacLaine Downes asked pleasantly.

"Of course not," Jeff replied for everybody.

MacLaine Downes turned his brilliant smile on Monica. "How are you, my dear?"

"I'm fine, Governor."

"It's good to see you back in Washington, even if it is for something as disagreeable and boring as finances," he jested, seating himself with grand grace opposite Monica at the polished table. "Your sojourn in the west has done wonders for you, my dear. You look marvelous."

"Thank you, Governor," Monica said, remembering to return his smile, "but you were always a notorious flatterer."

Somebody handed MacLaine Downes a copy of the report and the meeting droned on, until Jeff and the governor put their heads together and talked something over in quiet tones, nodding to the members of the committee. Then they glanced down the long table at Monica. "I don't think we need to ask you any more questions, Ms. Lewis," Jeff pronounced. "Thank you for your cooperation." He started to gather his papers in a neat pile. "The final deliberations won't take long, but I suggest you relax and perhaps even go to lunch. We'll let you know our decision when you return."

Monica kept her eyes focused on Jeff's hands as he manipulated the papers on the mahogany table. His fingers, long and tapered, seemed alive with barely contained agitation. Finally she looked up into his eyes. "If your deliberations won't take long, then I prefer to wait nearby for the verdict, Mr. Mac-Kennon." She couldn't help adding, "You know how important this is for my program, so I'm sure you'll understand that I'm too anxious to think of anything else at the moment."

Jeff wanted to say something else—she could see it in the glint of the dark eyes—but he kept silent and merely nodded. It was MacLaine Downes who took direct action by stepping over to Monica and lightly taking her elbow. "Of course, my dear, there's plenty of time for lunch after the suspense is over, right?" He guided her toward a side door. "Why don't you wait in this sitting room until the committee calls you?"

The room was small but as beautifully appointed as the main conference room. A few easy chairs and a desk were the only furnishings; a fireplace, flanked by a small leather sofa, added a touch of humanizing warmth. It was a room where people waited, in private anguish, for decisions that could make or break a civil-service career. Monica felt a great gratitude for MacLaine Downes's presence, realizing finally that his appearance at the meeting had been planned as a token of his support and compassion. "Governor," she said, looking across the small room to where he was still standing, "thank you for being here today. I needed your friendship. It was tough going in there," she admitted, nodding toward the conference room.

He immediately brushed away the importance of his appearance. "Jeff tells me that you had the committee eating out of your hand and panting to grant you the funds the moment you walked into the conference room yesterday," he laughed, with a wicked wink. "Don't fret, my dear, you'll get everything you want from those gentlemen now that you've made your request in person. I don't mind telling you that it was touch and go for a while—about waiting until next year to extend the grant, I mean."

"Then I'm glad I came to Washington," she said, feeling more at ease about the funding but feeling more and more miserable about the situation between herself and Jeff. "Anyway, I'm glad I had the opportunity to see you today, for a number of very good reasons—"

"Listen, my child, I don't want your thanks," the elder statesman interrupted. "Yes, I probably would have stuck my head in the door to say hello to you today, and, yes, I would have stopped by to gather a few notes for my monthly memo on educational matters for the President, but the main reason I dropped by today was that Jeff MacKennon insisted I come. As he put it, you needed a good friend by your side. Too bad that you can't put all your faith in *him*, because whether you know it or not, he's been your strongest, most loyal supporter."

At any other time and under different circumstances, she would have easily dissembled and replied with something acceptably vague until she'd had the time to decipher that odd statement. But she had been rocked by too much emotion and had faced too many critical problems in the past months. Her common sense and her iron will deserted her at that moment, and she heard herself blurt, "Oh, no, Governor, you're wrong! From the beginning, Jeff MacKennon has wanted to frustrate my every move. He *has* been wonderful about helping me with the funding, but that's his job, to help deserving educational projects— in every other way he's been selfish, insensitive to me, and. . . ." She swallowed. "Right from the start, Jeff MacKennon's concern was for himself, not for me and what I wanted to do."

"You're sadly mistaken," MacLaine Downes announced, shaking his head. "Monica, do you remember the last time we saw each other, when we talked about your plans and dreams?"

Nothing could ever make her forget that night. "Yes, it was at Marion Fairmont's party. A few weeks later, because you so graciously recommended me to Sacramento, I left Washington."

MacLaine Downes reached around to open the door, preparing to take his leave. "You're giving credit to the wrong person, my dear."

"That's impossible."

"Oh, it's true that I contacted your department in California—but I did it only after Jeff MacKennon pressured me into doing it." He watched as Monica's face changed with one fleeting emotion after another. *"He* was directly responsible for your move to California, not me. As to why he did it," the elder statesman added as he left the room, "I suggest that you get the answer from him. Good-bye, my dear, and good luck, always. . . ."

A long time afterward, she walked to the window. Traffic was heavy below, and the various noises rising from the broad streets of the busy capital easily invaded the solitude of the small waiting room. She stared through the window, seeing and hearing nothing. The only thing she was aware of was in her own mind, as she admitted a simple truth: *I've been so blind.*

Jeff found her seemingly mesmerized by the panorama of Washington on a clear, beautiful day. "Monica?" He waited for her to turn around. "The committee has reached a decision. The funds have been granted and the money will be forwarded to your department as quickly as possible so that you can start your youth program this summer." He stopped, anticipating a reaction that never happened. "You surprise me, Monica. I thought you'd be shouting for joy." Again he waited. "This was what you wanted, wasn't it? You've won, and now you have everything."

She was listening to him, but she was more intent on looking at him than on fully appreciating what he had just said. Perhaps it was only a trick of the light, she told herself, but the silver in his hair seemed to have increased since the last time she'd seen him. For some reason, this fact tugged at her heart. "I'm ecstatic about the funding," she finally replied sincerely, "and I'm also so relieved that I feel like crying and laughing like a crazy person." But only the mistiness in her blue eyes proved that she was telling the truth; her voice, the tilt of her chin, and her poise never wavered. "But over and above everything else, I hope you realize that I can never thank you enough for your assistance, Jeff."

He shrugged away her gratitude. "What I did was part of my job. You used your intelligence and expertise to create a model program and you would have received the money to continue your work somehow, somewhere. I know it."

"How strange!" She smiled quizzically, gazing at him. "At first, you were dead set against my so-called adventures in the wild west, but now you have nothing but praise for the work I'm doing." Her gaze increased in puzzlement. "Perhaps somewhere down the line you've forgotten to tell me something very important, Jeff, something which will explain your sudden change of mind."

"No, there's nothing."

"I think there is," she protested—and then came right to the point. "Why did you—and not MacLaine Downes, who was actually just an intermediary—personally assure my appointment in California?"

"So you finally found out," he said suddenly sounding defeated. He wasn't calm, now; he was very shaken. "I'm disappointed in the Governor. I thought he was the type of person who would keep a promise."

"Don't be too harsh with him," she replied. "Everybody has a moment of weakness, you know. I suppose it was my fault that he broke his promise to you never to tell me. But let's forget the Governor for the moment. Jeff, I want an answer from you and I want it right now. Why did you keep it a secret from me?"

He waited an interminable amount of time before answering. "I knew you'd resent it, terribly." He prevented her fast denial with an impatient snap of his head. "You may not admit it, even now, but at the time you came off as having a great big chip on your shoulder. You didn't want help from anybody, especially me."

"I never had a chip on my shoulder!"

"All mavericks do, to some extent," he shot back, but then he tried to retrieve his usual calmness. "But please, let's not get into a hassle about semantics.

Let's say that you've made your point about being completely independent and you can take great pride in doing a fine job all by yourself. You were right then and you're right now—you're completely self-sufficient."

"And yet, you put pressure on the Governor to finally send off that recommendation, didn't you? If that's the way you saw me then—blindly independent and self-sufficient—*why did you do it?*"

He moved closer. "Because I wanted you to go to California and then come back to Washington with all that nonsense out of your system."

She jumped to interrupt him. "Oh, you did, did you?"

"That's right," he said, finally showing some of the exasperation he felt at himself. "I wanted you to come back to me, but now I know it was for the wrong reason."

"So I was to come back whimpering, and then I was to take a number and get in line with the rest of your groupies, is that it?"

"Perhaps," he stated with disarming honesty, "but I meant *every* word I said, right from the beginning, about hoping you would begin to practice law."

"While I hung around town and climbed into bed with you when the spirit moved you, huh?"

"But only if the spirit moved you, too, remember?"

His voice had dropped to a dangerous low. She was being warned not to push him much harder; he was demanding that she admit that her responses had been as sensual, swift and overt as his. Okay, that much was true, but the rest still irked her. "So what happened to change your game plan, Jeff MacKennon?"

"Why don't you stop being so melodramatic and give me a chance to explain?" He suddenly smiled in a way that scoffed at his own thoughts. "Don't worry, I won't try to convince you that I was right and you were wrong. If anything, everything's turned around."

She nodded after a moment and then sat down on the nearest chair. "Go ahead, Jeff." Leaning back, she hoped that she appeared levelheaded and tranquil. Actually, she was prepared to run from the room before he suspected that her heart was beating like a drum gone wild. "I'm listening."

He closed his eyes for a second and rubbed his temples; his next movement was to walk to the window and gaze at the city beyond. "Do you remember the night we were in Marion Fairmont's library? At her party, when MacLaine Downes wanted me to talk to the men from the White House?"

At the ironic mention of that evening for the second time today, she almost laughed aloud in bitterness. But all she said was, "Yes, I remember it very well."

"That was when I began to understand you, I think," he said, concentrating on the wide streets below and the stately buildings and monuments in the distance. He was looking, urgently, at everything but *her*. "I started to realize that you had suffered a lot when the Governor slipped up and mentioned it, and afterward, when I held you—when you *let me hold you*," he corrected himself, recalling the gentleness of that moment, "I knew that there was something very special about you, something that got to me. Maybe it was the way you could be so strong and yet so unsure of yourself, both at the same time. Then later that night, I cornered MacLaine Downes—"

"Before or after you talked to the President's men?" she insisted on knowing.

He turned to face her, but he stayed by the window and didn't move a step closer. "I never got the chance to talk to them that night. Instead, I spent the evening questioning the Governor about you."

"You did?" She bent forward in surprise, intent on his every word. "And the members of the White House staff . . . ?"

"I spoke to them a few days later, as part of a deal I made with MacLaine Downes." There was a trace of a smile on his face. "But I thought I was supposed to talk and you were supposed to listen."

"Yes, I'm sorry, go on."

"After you left the library, I went to find the staff members, but the Governor, visibly upset, informed me that they had become impatient waiting for me—"

"While you were in the library with me, being so darned nice."

"And they had gone," he finished smoothly, ignoring her words. "The funny thing was, I should have been upset, too, but I wasn't," he confessed, able to smile at the incident now. "I still had you on my mind, not politics. A bit out of character for Jeff MacKennon, wouldn't you say?"

"Please . . ."

"So, instead, I soothed the Governor's feathers and dragged him off to a quiet spot in the house and made him talk about you. Since he had no choice, he told me a few details about your past. That's how I found out what happened to your husband, but the Governor didn't say anything about the baby you'd lost."

"Nobody knew about it," she murmured, with fragile irony, "except my father, who had to rush me to the hospital."

Jeff deliberately waited to go on, and when he did, his words were soft. "Well, I suppose I acted on impulse, but that's when I made my deal with Mac-Laine Downes. I promised that I would eat crow and apologize to the White House staff for not showing up, and then I swore I would make a definite appointment to talk to them—the Governor beamed because he saw himself in the role of kingmaker—in exchange for his immediate recommendation that you get the job in Sacramento."

Perched on the edge of her chair, she demanded, "So you made a deal, with yourself as bait, just so that I could get a lot of 'nonsense' out of my system?"

"I guess I wanted you to realize that you couldn't force me out of your life. That being self-sufficient didn't automatically mean that you could be immune to caring about another person again. That's the nonsense I was talking about. It made a lot of sense to me at the time. I felt good about it, and I began to feel that you *could* become a part of my life." Having admitted that much, he felt a compulsion to add, "But I didn't go to California to stroke my ego, hoping to find that you were miserable over missing me. I just wanted to see you again, and I wanted to see for myself if you were happy. But you pushed me away, as stubborn and hardheaded as ever."

"What else could I do?" she replied. "You kept testing me. Even when we said good-bye at the airport you had to have the last word!"

"I felt desperate and defeated and I said something very stupid, okay? I admit it," he conceded in a monotone, folding his arms across his chest with stoic finality. "You told me about your unhappiness with your marriage and I finally understood why you would never again go through that hell, *not even with me,* not even after you said you loved me, not even after I believed you. All right, so now we've both proved our points. You're still a maverick and I'm still obsessed with my career, and we've both managed to mess up our lives by accidentally falling in love. But as you keep reminding me, nothing has changed and we'll survive, right?"

Monica realized that she had been holding her breath. Without a word, she got up from the chair, crossed the room, and then threw her arms around his neck. She felt him grow rigid with surprise as he hesitated, arms still crossed, to reach for her. She panicked for a second. However, when he slowly, very slowly, began to pull her closer, she knew the battle was half-won. "I've been listening to you, and now I want you to shut up and listen to me," she whispered, pressing her mouth against his chest so that the words fluttered through his clothes and caressed his skin. "Everything has changed. Sure, I'll always be stubborn as hell, and I'll always get what I want, and by god, *I want you.*" She felt his fingers press into her shoulders, mutely but lovingly telling her better than mere words that he couldn't let her go either; it gave her the strength to persist. "We'd darned well better find a solution, and, darling, I can only think of *one.*"

"If it beats spending half our lives on planes trying to get together," he groaned, "I want to hear it."

"I can come back to Washington." She felt his body twist in protest. "No, please listen to me! Holly will make a very fine director for the youth programs, especially now that she'll have the funding to work with, so I can leave Sacramento knowing that I really did accomplish something after all, don't you see?" She lifted her mouth and kissed the objections from his lips. "And I won't be unhappy here, not if you love me. I won't mope around. I'll go to work. I might even practice law."

"You make a poor liar, you know," he murmured, bending his head to find her mouth and stop her protests. But this time he didn't let her get away with a slight brush of a kiss. They clung together, because they had been apart too long and they had hurt each other too deeply and they were starving for each other. But he finally pulled away to speak. "I love you, and I couldn't stand by and watch you live a life you've always hated—the party scenes, the struggles to survive in this city, the political jungle—just for my sake. No, darling, I have a much better idea."

"A sudden impulse?" she joked, hoping he would never know how much it had cost her to offer to return to the past.

"Call it a growing inspiration," he suggested, expertly reading her mind and wanting to let the past stay buried. He framed her face with his hands and smiled down at her. "Maybe it started when I kept that appointment at the White House and suddenly turned down the offer to join the administration. For the first time in my life, I didn't want to conform. Suddenly I thought of you—and I almost choked in the stale air." His fingers smoothed away the questions that narrowed her eyes. "I think I could learn to like breathing the clean air out there in your wild west."

"And your future—your career?" He had managed to shock her before, but it was nothing compared to this. "No, Jeff, it won't work!"

"It will," he laughed. "I always know exactly what I'm doing, remember? I'll prove to you that contracts can be very important. I've been offered a high-ranking post in Sacramento, and I think I'm going to accept it."

She could only whisper, "California . . . after you've turned down a post at the White House?"

"The White House position was political, while the job in Sacramento will be as a liaison between the local California agencies and the federal agencies in Washington. In short, darling, there are no strings attached. I'll be free to plan a future doing what I've always wanted to do—seek an elective office."

"You're serious, aren't you?" she asked, awed by the determination she saw in his face. "You really are serious about this!"

"I am. What's more, I have plans for you, too."

"Plans? What plans?"

"With your background in law, do you think—by the time I'm ready to enter an election and if your very important work with youth programs permits—that you might be interested in managing my campaign?"

"Interested?" Her legs finally gave out. She pulled away and sank onto the small leather sofa which thankfully was nearby. "Jeff MacKennon, I would be thrilled to be your campaign manager!"

He leaned over her. "That leaves only one last question, Monica."

He was moving too fast for her, and she felt light-headed. "It does?"

"Shall we get married here immediately, or wait until we settle down together in California?"

"Can't I have some time to think about it?" she asked as he slipped down next to her.

"Sure, I'll give you thirty seconds."

"That's enough time, actually." She stroked his shoulder, thinking very deeply. "Here, I think, but maybe not so immediately. Let's not put too much pressure on Marion Fairmont," she declared, slipping her arms around him. "Let's give her a few days to organize all the details."

"Just a moment." He leaned away so that he could look her straight in the eye. "What does Marion Fairmont have to do with our wedding?"

"Oh, we're not going to have a prim-and-proper little ceremony in somebody's little garden, you know. Oh, no! I'm going to marry you at the grandest bash this town's ever seen, and Marion will throw one of her greatest parties for us. You don't mind, darling, do you?"

"No," he murmured, slightly baffled, "but why?"

"Just mark it down to a feminine whim."

"Monica," he objected, but not too strongly, mainly because he was more interested at the moment in the way her body was softly yielding everywhere he touched it, "I've never known you to give in to a whim. You're too stubborn and strong-minded."

"Just this once, then?" she coaxed, starting to feel very good all over. "I want everybody who is anybody in this city to know that I've nabbed you."

"Everybody . . . ?"

"Half the female population, anyway," she stated without a vestige of shame. "Then when we return to Sacramento, we can have another party with Holly and Gavin. I know a perfect place in the old-town section for a little celebration."

"Where?" he wanted to know, almost afraid to ask.

"A great Mexican restaurant that serves fantastic tacos and super piña coladas." She took pity on him. "You've been so wonderful agreeing with everything I want that I'll do you a favor in return, darling."

"I can't wait to hear what it is."

"I promise to distract Father tonight every time he launches into one of his dry judicial monologues over supper."

"Supper . . . tonight—with your father?"

"I'm afraid so," she murmured, arching her neck to show him the exact spot, at the base of her throat, where she yearned to be kissed. "He invited me, earlier, and I really can't disappoint him. But now you can come, too, and we can tell him we're getting married."

"Hm-m-m," he moaned in distracted agreement, "but we have hours and hours before we meet your father for supper, haven't we?"

She understood perfectly, but she had only one small doubt. "Here . . . ?"

"I'm still one of the directors of this agency and nobody would dare to enter this room without knocking," he informed her in a whisper. "Anyway, I locked the door when I came in."

"In that case, darling . . ."

Until that moment, the small sitting room in the vast Capitol Building had been the scene of a variety of dry political skirmishes and a few unemotional agreements culminating in impersonal handshakes. Now, however, it was about to be an inanimate witness to the start of a consummate and enduring and sensational love affair.

Silhouette Desire

AUGUST TITLES

THE DEVIL TO PAY
Stephanie James

THE TENDER BARBARIAN
Dixie Browning

STARSTRUCK LOVERS
Suzanne Michelle

THE BEST REASONS
Beverly Bird

CAPITOL AFFAIR
Fran Bergen

MORE THAN PROMISES
Amanda Lee

Four New
Silhouette Romances
could be yours
ABSOLUTELY FREE

Did you know that Silhouette Romances are no longer available from the shops in the U.K?

Read on to discover how you could receive four brand new Silhouette Romances, **free** and **without obligation,** with this special introductory offer to the new Silhouette Reader Service.

As thousands of women who have read these books know — Silhouette Romances sweep you away into an exciting love filled world of fascination between men and women. A world filled with

age-old conflicts — love and money, ambition and guilt, jealousy and pride, even life and death.

Silhouette Romances are the latest stories written by the world's best romance writers, and they are **only** available from Silhouette Reader Service. Take out a subscription and you could receive 6 brand new titles every month, plus a newsletter bringing you all the latest information from Silhouette's New York editors. All this delivered in one exciting parcel direct to your door, with no charges for postage and packing.

And at only 95p for a book, Silhouette Romances represent the very best value in Romantic Reading.

Remember, Silhouette Romances are **only** available to subscribers, so don't miss out on this very special opportunity. Fill in the certificate below and post it today. You don't even need a stamp.

- ✂ - - -

FREE BOOK CERTIFICATE

To: Silhouette Reader Service, FREEPOST, P.O. Box 236, Croydon, Surrey. CR9 9EL

Readers in South Africa—write to:
Silhouette Romance Club, Private Bag X3010, Randburg 2125.

Yes, please send me, free and without obligation, four brand new Silhouette Romances and reserve a subscription for me. If I decide to subscribe, I shall receive six brand new books every month for £5.70 , post and packing free. If I decide not to subscribe I shall write to you within 10 days. The free books are mine to keep, whatever I decide. I understand that I may cancel my subscription at any time simply by writing to you. I am over 18 years of age. Please write in BLOCK CAPITALS.

Signature _____

Name _____

Address _____

_____ Postcode _____

SEND NO MONEY — TAKE NO RISKS.
Please don't forget to include your Postcode.

Remember postcodes speed delivery. Offer applies in U K only and is not valid to present subscribers. Silhouette reserve the right to exercise discretion in granting membership. If price changes are necessary you will be notified. Offer expires December 1985.

EPS1

Silhouette Desire

Your chance to write back!

We'll send you details of an exciting free offer from *SILHOUETTE*, if you can help us by answering the few simple questions below.

Just fill in this questionnaire, tear it out and put it in an envelope and post today to: Silhouette Reader Survey, FREEPOST, P.O. Box 236, Croydon, Surrey CR9 9EL. You don't even need a stamp.

What is the title of the *SILHOUETTE Desire* you have just read?

_____

How much did you enjoy it?

Very much ☐   Quite a lot ☐   Not very much ☐

Would you buy another *SILHOUETTE Desire* book?

Yes ☐   Possibly ☐   No ☐

How did you discover *SILHOUETTE Desire* books?

Advertising ☐   A friend ☐   Seeing them on sale ☐

Elsewhere (please state) _____

How often do you read romantic fiction?

Frequently ☐   Occasionally ☐   Rarely ☐

Name (Mrs/Miss) _____

Address _____

_____

_____ **Postcode** _____

Age group: Under 24 ☐   25–34 ☐   35–44 ☐

45–55 ☐   Over 55 ☐

Silhouette Reader Service, P.O. Box 236, Croydon, Surrey CR9 9EL.
Readers in South Africa—write to:
Silhouette Romance Club,
Private Bag X3010, Randburg 2125.

SDI